Leonard

BLOOD BROTHERHOOD BOOK 3

KATHI S. BARTON

World Castle Publishing, LLC
Pensacola, Florida

Copyright © Kathi S. Barton 2015
Hardback ISBN: 9781629893273
Print ISBN: 9781629893280
eBook ISBN: 9781629893297
First Edition World Castle Publishing, LLC, September 7, 2015
http://www.worldcastlepublishing.com

Cover: Karen Fuller
Editor: Eric Johnston
Editor: Maxine Bringenberg

Dedication

I dedicate this book to my street team, Team Barton.

Ladies, it means a great deal to me that I can call on you any time I need you, even if it's not book related or to just have a good laugh (which I have to admit, means more to me than you can imagine). I could not have done this without not just your support in pimping me and making me look good but your undying friendship as well. You are by and far the best group of women I know.

Thank you. Thank you from the bottom of my heart for being there when I need you. Making me laugh when I wanted to cry and sending me into fits of laughter when you teased me. Simply said, I could not have gotten where I am without you all. Thank you.

I love you each and every one of you,

Love, your friend Kathi

Chapter 1

Waking to the sound of the alarm nearly had her screaming. CarolAnn turned the noisy thing off and lay there trying to remember why she'd set it. Then with a squeal, she jumped out of bed and ran to her closet. She was seeing the lawyer today.

Several weeks ago she'd gone to the hospital to have Leonard sign off on a will she'd had made for him, after not seeing him for a couple of weeks. She'd thought he'd be so close to death by then that he'd be drugged up and she could get him to do whatever she wanted. But he was gone. It took her several hours to get any information and was finally told that he'd left on his own several weeks ago. CarolAnn didn't think that was right for some reason.

Picking out her dress with care, she made her way to the shower to get ready. Glad now that she'd contacted someone right away to get this settled, she was excited to see how much he'd left her. She knew that he'd had a change of heart by now and couldn't wait to cash it in. There was no way that he'd leave her with nothing after all the time she'd spent with him before he became ill. There was no way he'd just leave her hanging.

CarolAnn hadn't really wanted to marry Leonard in the first place. He'd been nice enough; great in bed, but he wasn't rich. Not even close. And her plan had been to marry well and often. Leonard had been the only one of all the men she'd known to ask her, however, and she was getting tired of waiting around for the right man to come along. Then he'd gotten that fucking illness and had ruined everything. But there had to be insurance, and that would go a long way to helping her look good to potential husband material.

It had taken her over a week to decide that marrying Leo, after he'd told her that he was going to die, would be hard on her. She'd had someone look it up, this thing he'd let himself get, and the way he was going to die — because there was no way he'd not — was long and drawn out. And it would be consuming of her time. Who wanted to be married to a person that was going to be so sick and so weak that there would be nothing for them to do but to sit around and be together? She was young. Beautiful. And he was going to drag her away from her fun. That, of course, was why she wanted to marry anyway, to have fun without anyone thinking she was a whore.

Not for the first time she wondered where her staff was in the house that she had lived in since birth. Not that she had that many, but her sister usually came by at least twice a day to check on her and to pick up after her. CarolAnn knew that she owed Alice a great deal of money for her working for her, but she'd been in a slump and there wasn't much to spend on things like domestic help. Besides, as her sister, she should be glad to do those things for her big sister and not get paid. Alice had nothing better to do than work anyway, and CarolAnn loved it when she came to her house and fussed with her pretty things.

Going out to her car, she was glad to see it sitting where she'd left it. Those bank people had called her several times over the last few weeks, and the last man had left her a nasty message telling her that they were going to take it back should she not make arrangements to pay the five months she was behind.

"Like I have that sort of money. And even if I did, this car isn't that nice anyway." Smiling, she thought of all the things she was going to do with the insurance money. First and foremost, she was getting a new outfit. Then get her hair and nails done. Looking at the chipped polish she had on them now, she would have to remember to keep her hands hidden from Dillon. Her lawyer, Dillon Marshall, was someone on her list of very fuckable men that she wanted to marry.

Sitting in the waiting room to go back and talk to him, she decided that having a lawyer as a husband would open so many doors for her. She'd be the envy of everyone she knew and even people she didn't know. The fact that he was married didn't bother her very much. CarolAnn knew how to fuck that up too. When his secretary told her she could go back, she straightened her dress and moved toward the office.

The woman who had shown her in didn't like her. There were all kinds of reasons why she shouldn't, but right now CarolAnn didn't really care. She supposed that she shouldn't have been nasty to her on the phone the few times she'd called to talk to Dillon, but CarolAnn could find no earthly reason why she of all people shouldn't be able to call Dillon at home. She was his most important client, CarolAnn had told her, and those kind of clients deserved his home number. When she entered his office, she was disappointed to find him not alone but with three other people.

"Have a seat, Miss Rivas. And before we begin, I want to inform you that this entire meeting is being recorded." She smiled at him and told him again to call her by her first name. "This is my partner Marvin Foster, and this is Doctor Peter Gault. I think you know him. He was the man treating your fiancé. These men are here for two reasons. One, that we have witnesses to what I'm about to tell you. And they are experts in the case of Mr. Leo Earl. We have a few questions for you."

Smiling broadly at them, she told them to go ahead. "His name is Leonard Earl, not Leo. That sounds too much like a dog or some animal. But I have to warn you, I've been away for some time on personal business. I don't know where Leonard is buried or any of the details of his death. So if you have any of that information, I would greatly appreciate it."

She'd not been anywhere really but hiding from bill collectors. Also, a few times she'd tried to follow Dillon home, but that had never worked out the way it seemed to always do in the movies. It was hard following someone.

Pulling out her hankie, she wiped delicately at her eyes, careful as always of her make-up and her hair. She might be a gold digger, but she was a pretty one and wanted to make sure that everyone could see that she took care of herself.

"Miss Rivas, Leo isn't dead." She looked around the room. Surely this was a joke. But the doctor nodded as he continued. "We had been giving him a great deal of pain meds up until the morning of the tenth, and when the nurse went in to check his vitals, she fully expected him to be...well, gone. But he was better. I mean, he was in perfect health other than some oddities with his temperature; but he's not dead."

"You're not very nice. And that's simply not possible. He told me that he was dying and that this cancer thing was going to kill him. You even told us that." The doctor nodded and looked at the other two men. "What's really going on here? Leonard is dead. I know that. You told me that he was going to die. He was leaving me his insurance. I'm here to collect on it. He would have left it all to me as his fiancée."

"No. He didn't leave you anything. Not even...there is a will, but we didn't find any insurance policy. Not that anyone could collect on it, as he's not passed away yet. But his will cannot be read until such time as a record of his death is made. And there isn't one. As I have said, Leo Earl is not dead." A paper was slid her way and she stared at it without reading as her lawyer continued. "That is a copy of the discharge papers that were given to Leo the day he left the hospital. As you can see, that's his signature at the bottom. As well as that of his doctor and the attending nurse. They all signed—"

"No, Leonard is dead." Dillon shook his head and then the other guy started talking. She cut him off by slamming her hand down on the table that they were seated at. "I don't want to hear about the miracle of his recovery. There is no recovery for him. He is dead. And as such, he left me his money. Now if you think this is funny, I assure you that it's not. Give me my money and I'll forget about you and me becoming man and wife. I no longer think that we'd be suited."

"You and I are never going to be...I've gone over this with you before, Miss Rivas. I'm married...happily; and there is no us. There is no money because he didn't die to have any insurance policy validated. And in the event that you don't understand, had he had an insurance policy—which again, he did not—you could not collect on it because he is not dead." CarolAnn stood up and the door behind her opened and closed. Dillon stood as well. "Miss Rivas, these men are going to help you out. We're finished here."

"No. We will be finished when I say so. And I want my money. Every penny of it." Someone touched her from behind. Jerking from the hands that touched her, she leaned on the table. "Get your fucking checkbook and pay me. Now, damn it. I'm not fucking around here."

Before she could say anything else, CarolAnn found herself on the floor. The man that was holding her down was pushing her head down so hard she felt the fibers in the carpet cut into her face. And trying to get up did no good; she was down where he wanted her. After a few minutes she was helped up, but she wasn't able to do anything but what they directed her to do, and that was to move toward the door. A man on either side of her held her arms so that she couldn't reach out and slap the piss right out of Dillon and the other men. This was just not fair.

As soon as she was on the sidewalk, she was let go. Her purse was handed to her, as were her keys and jacket. CarolAnn tried to muscle her way back in but only succeeded in messing up her hair. This was not the way she had envisioned her day.

She was walking to the parking garage when she saw her car leaving it on the back of a flat-bedded truck.

"Wait, that's my car." The man only nodded at her and told her to move. CarolAnn stepped in front of the slow-moving truck when he stopped at a stop sign. "You can't just take my car. How the hell will I get around?"

"Lady, I don't care if you have to walk to the end of the earth from now on. Get your fat ass out of my way and let me get on with my job." When he gunned the engine, she nearly screamed and then fell back. Standing up again didn't stop him because he just drove around her. CarolAnn was still staring after her car when someone touched her on the shoulder.

"Miss Rivas?" CarolAnn nodded at the gorgeous man. "This is for you. And you've been served. Your eviction notice for your Maple Street residence has been duly served to you, and as of now, everything within the house is the property of the bank and will be sold at auction to try and recoup their losses."

CarolAnn looked around. When she saw the law office she'd been in, she looked at the secretary standing there with Dillon. They were both laughing at her. And she knew in that moment that they'd done this…set her up so that she would lose everything. Going to the window, she pounded on it and was happy to see them back up.

"I'll get you for this. See if I don't." They only laughed harder, and she flipped them off. Fuck them. She was going home and taking a nice long soak in her tub, then she would find Leonard. This was his fault. If he had just died like he said he was going to, then she'd be rich right now. CarolAnn had always prided herself on the fact that she got what she wanted. And Leonard's insurance was it.

~~~

Pulling her bow to her cheek, she watched the man going into the little shop. Jamey had been sitting there for an hour, picking off the weird guys one at a time. It wasn't really as much fun as it had been at first…now it was simply something to do. And lately there were a lot of weird things going on that she could see.

13

Letting the arrow slip through her fingers, she watched it nail the guy in the head. When he fell to the ground, Jamey pulled another arrow out and waited. There was little doubt that she'd have another target in no time. And as of the moment she had turned sixteen, she'd had more arrows than she could ever use, and her bow and quiver were always on her.

Jamey had been pretty good at archery for a long time. She'd first picked up the bow and arrow set that had belonged to her dad when she was about six. It had been way too big for her little body, but he'd gotten her one when she begged for over a month that she'd like to do it. Dad wasn't really very keen on his little girl doing archery. He'd never been very good at it, he told her later, and he didn't want her to fail at it too. But she'd been good, really good, and he'd taken her to all kinds of events after that.

She was a champ, and had won more trophies in her short career than most did in their entire life. After she'd won all the regions she could, gotten medal after medal in state competitions, she'd gone out for the big game. The Olympics.

But things had happened. Her coach was convicted of child pornography and she was questioned. Things went from her being on top of the world to her being thought of as a lure for the man. He told the courts he'd used her, and that she had agreed to bring him children to play with. Jamey had been examined, prodded, and made to look like she'd done something wrong, terribly wrong. Her father, her biggest fan, had sent her out into the cold world and had killed himself. The shame, he told her in a note, had been more than he could handle. Then all of this started happening.

The first time she'd seen one of the weird people was the day of her dad's funeral. She'd not been where anyone could see her at the graveside services...Jamey had caused her dad enough grief without showing up at his funeral too. But she'd seen him, the man standing so close to her aunt that she wanted to warn her. Then three days later her aunt was one of them too.

People all over the town were changing. Dogs and cats had been changed too, but they didn't last as long as the people. Faded out children were running around and touching people until they too, were changed. The children lasted about as long as the animals, not having a clue of what to do to survive in a world that killed for the sake of killing. And through it all, Jamey had never been affected by the touch.

They had touched her too, lots of times and everywhere, until one day, out of the blue, they were afraid of her...terrified to the point where they would run screaming. Two such weirdos had even killed themselves when she'd cornered them to ask them what had changed. Soon after that she found the mark on her shoulder.

It was a sort of half dragon. The voice in her head had told her that it was his mark and that she'd have it forever. She knew that he was a dragon as well, the voice, but she'd never seen him. But he'd been with her since she'd been old enough to realize that she wasn't alone in her body. He'd kept her company all these past years.

The woman coming out of the little shop made her pause. Jamey had seen her a few times over the last few weeks, coming and going out of different buildings close to here, and wondered why she hadn't been approached by the weird people. A couple of times she'd been with a big guy, but mostly she was alone. Today, however, she came toward Jamey.

Jamey sat still. She was high enough in the tree that nothing would get to her until she got down. And the woman had no ladder or any other means of getting to her, so Jamey just waited. When the woman was beneath her, looking right up, Jamey looked back at her.

"Hello." Not answering her, Jamey pulled another arrow from her quiver and held it ready. "You're the one that has been picking off the malefactors, aren't you?"

"Is that what they're called?" The woman nodded. "I don't bother the ones that are in color. Those I figure are okay. But that doesn't mean I won't kill anyone that tries anything."

"You mean me." It wasn't a question, but Jamey nodded anyway. "Okay. Good to know. But I don't want to bother you, not really. I'd like to offer you a job."

"Sure you would. And you'll pay me in gold doubloons and checks that'll bounce so much I'll be chasing them for a month. No thanks." Another malefactor started for the shop and she killed him. The woman watched him fall over before looking up at her. "I'm just fine on my own. They don't bother me and I kill as many as I can."

"That's what I do...we do. We're a group of people trying our best to rid the world of these guys. I'd like to offer you a place to stay and a job. It pays with real money." Another malefactor came down the street toward them. Jamey pulled another arrow out, but the woman lifted her hand and the thing just disappeared in a puff of white light. "I'm going to come up there to talk to you. I'm drawing too much attention just being down here."

Before Jamey could tell her no, she sprouted wings and came up the side of the tree with a short burst of movement from them. Jamey moved back when she asked her to scoot over, and when she sat down, Jamey pointed her bow at her.

"I don't know what the fuck you are, but you'd better get away from me right now." The woman only pushed the arrow down and smiled. Jamey wasn't sure what to do when the woman started talking.

"I'm Skylar. My mate's name is Remy. Well, Rembrandt, but we call him Remy. Your name is Jamey, right?" Nodding, she put her arrow and bow on her lap but didn't let go of either. "I'm an immortal. I'm sure there are ways to kill me eventually, but you shooting me is just going to piss me off, and I have high hopes that we'll be friends."

"Why?" Skylar laughed. "This isn't funny. If you'd seen the shit I have, you'd be hiding out, not fucking shooting the bull with me."

"See? I knew there was a reason to like you. You didn't ask me how I flew up here. No, you were ready to protect me." Jamey had no idea how she'd come to that conclusion, but she waited. "There are a lot of things going on everywhere, and while I'm sure that you've seen more than most, I don't think you've seen as much as I have. And we're still trying to figure this out too."

"How did you fly up here? I mean, I saw the wings, but where did you get those?" Skylar looked down when a car came to the street, and Jamey looked too. She knew that car. It was one of the ones that this woman had been in. "You need to go, and I'd very much like it if you didn't blab about me. I'm not into people anymore."

"You're outnumbered. They're going to find you before long and when they do, they'll hurt you and change you." Jamey didn't say anything, but Skylar turned to her with a frown. "You have been touched by them, haven't you? They...you're immune to it."

"I don't know what you mean." But she did and Skylar knew it. When her wings spread out again, Jamey waited for her to grab her and take her against her will. But she only looked down at the man below them, then back at her.

"We won't hurt you. And we'd really like for you to join us." Jamey told her no thanks. "All right then. There's a building about three miles south of here. It's usually surrounded by malefactors, but there is a shield around it that keeps the building and all that live there safe. If you change your mind, just come there and I'll make sure you have what you need."

"I don't need anything. I'm doing fine on my own." Skylar leapt off the limb they were sharing and hovered in the air. "I'll move on if you want. I know that you're trying to get the grid up and going, but you're in the wrong building."

"Where is the one we need, please? We want to open some of the buildings and have power go to them." Jamey pointed to the little building about a hundred yards from them. "That's only a substation."

"It's what it's supposed to look like. When you open the door, there's a green switch and a blue one. Don't touch the blue one, but the green one is a key. Turn it to the left." She'd used the same kind of small building when she'd moved into the neighborhood she was in now. The house had been abandoned some months ago, she supposed, and had taken it. "Use the key like you would a regular house key and open the box in the substation. Once you have it open, push the blue button. I have no idea why that works, but it sort of resets things."

Skylar thanked her, and she and the man went to the small housing box. In minutes Jamey could see that the power was back on in the buildings all around them. With a thumbs up, Skylar and the man left her still sitting in the tree as they drove off in the large car.

Jamey didn't have wings to get out of the tree but she did have something else...a power that at first had scared her to death. But she'd been assured that while it was going to help her, she wouldn't be harmed by it. He'd made a promise to her.

And true to his word, the more she used it, the more comfortable she got with it, until now it was as much a part of her as her bow and arrow were. Calling on it, she was lifted from the tree and sat gently on the ground. Jamey was moving toward her bike when she realized that she was going to have more neighbors now that there was power to the stores.

Jamey rode the bike, the biggest one she could find, all the way to the other side of town to find a store that had been ransacked about two weeks ago. There were still things on the shelf, mostly canned goods, but she took what she wanted. By the time she was finished with her shopping, it was getting pretty dark. She put everything in the bags on the side of the bike and rode across town to her home

The food was put away in about twenty minutes. Some of the things she had she just lay out on the counter to be taken should someone break in. Twice before now she'd been robbed of her food, and it was annoying to clean up after people. She knew it was humans that had taken her things because so far as she'd seen, the only thing the malefactors ate was human flesh. Going to the basement,

Jamey pulled up her computer after she'd locked herself in the bomb shelter that had done the owners of it no good.

Jamey made notes on her day in the diary she'd created on the computer, including how many of the things she'd killed and the fact that she'd met Skylar. It took her some time to decide if she should write that the woman had wings. But she finally thought what the fuck, it was hers and no one else was going to read it but her.

At midnight she locked herself inside with the large bar across the door and crawled into bed. The food that she'd gotten today for her was stashed away, the refrigerator was full, and if she ever wanted to, she could have planted herself some vegetables in the hydro garden that she'd gotten up and running a few days ago. These people had been really serious about their shelter.

Closing her eyes, she saw him and wondered if he really looked like that or if it was her mind that made him so real...the dragon that had been a part of her life since she'd been about six. But only in that he'd talk to her. Now she could not just speak to him, but see him too. He moved around in her vison and she wanted to assure him that she was fine, but he never believed her and she rarely tried any more. When he finally lay down, she spoke to him.

"Skylar? Do you know her?" He lifted his head and sniffed the air, but she knew better than to rush him. "She has wings. Not like yours, but she has them all the same."

Her mate is Rembrandt. Jamey told him that was right. The dragon knew everything, but he would only tell her what he wanted her to know. *He is there. The man that owns me. He is there.*

Jamey didn't let out the breath that seemed to be clogged in her lungs. The dragon had been telling her about a man, one that owned him, for a month now. It was why she'd come to this part of the state. Why she was waiting every day for him to show himself.

"I'll take you to him if you know where he is." The dragon only lay there, looking at her with his great green eyes. "Do you?"

I do. So do you. She told him she had no idea where he was. *You met one of his kind today. Skylar. And on Wednesday, you will take me to him.*

She had five days. Five days to try and think how she was going to live without him there. He'd been her...ally, she supposed, all her life, and now she was supposed to give him to someone else. A man that owned him.

Jamey had no idea how this was supposed to work. She'd always thought that the dragon was a figment of her imagination. But now she knew better. He was as real as her. Bigger, stronger, and certainly smarter, but he was real. And now she had to give him up.

You will not be alone, Jamey of the Arrow. I will continue to protect you as always. Jamey nodded and rolled to her side. *Once you have met my owner, you will understand. He will be...he will be most unhappy with you and me, but it will be for the best.*

"Then why do you have to go to him?" No answer, not that she expected to get one. "I'll take you on Wednesday. And when I do, I'm going back to my apartment. I've had enough of traveling for you."

His laughter pissed her off, but she said nothing. Opening her eyes, she heard him laugh again and told him to fuck off. When sleep took her, she dreamt of a man who was cruel like no other and would harm her dragon.

Chapter 2

The store was cleaned out, but Leo had managed to find a warehouse loaded with foodstuff that had been put onto trucks that would never roll. Not by the owners anyway. He had no idea how to drive a big semi, but he was pretty sure that he could figure it out. It wasn't like he had to go that far, and there were few cars on the roads he'd have to travel anyway. Learning as he went wasn't anything new for him.

Four hours later, he was still in the yard where the warehouse was and he was no closer to figuring out how to drive than he'd been before. But he had managed to run over a vending machine that had been filled with soft drinks and a little cart that he was sure once ran up and down the long aisles of the place. It was crushed into a small splat on the ground, along with about fifty of the drinks.

"You having a good time?" He looked at Davis and thought about growling at him. He'd done that to Skylar once, and when he was able to move again, he decided that he'd not ever do that again. "I might be able to help you before this stuff expires."

"I think I have time to learn before then." Leo hated people. Not just the few that he worked with but all of them. And if he didn't need to be with them—and that was something he'd yet to figure out...this need—he'd be gone right now. "If you can do it, just fucking do it. I'm going to load the truck up with water and take it to the compound."

As he turned on the forklift, something that he'd had better luck with, he heard what sounded to him like something being run over and turned off the lift to listen. When nothing more came about, he went outside to see if Davis had hit something and was ready to make fun of him when he realized that he was alone. The truck was gone and the gates, which they'd been keeping locked since they'd started coming here, were locked as well. Davis was apparently good at that job as well. Then he heard it again.

The sky was dark with a storm and his first thought was that Benton was coming for him. Stepping back into the shelter of the building, he watched the skies to see if anything was around. Nothing. But he had a feeling that he wasn't looking in the right place. Or it was all in his head. Leo started back for the lift to load some water into the panel truck when he heard the voice.

You should know that we'll be there soon. The voice sounded so familiar and so strong that he looked around for the man. *I'm not out of my shell as yet, Master, but soon. Wednesday she will bring me to you.*

"Who the fuck is this?" He turned several times, trying to see everywhere at once, but only saw his shadows. Drawing his sword, he stood there waiting for anything that might come out. "Show yourself. Where are you?"

I am not there, Master, as I have told you. But soon. Leo felt his blood cool in his body. The voice laughed then. *You run hot now so that when I come to you, you'll be able to handle me. I will be a great addition to you.*

"You're a part of Remy's group? The men who fight with him." The laughter again. "I'm not fucking with you. I want you to show yourself to me or I'll run you through."

And how shall you do that when you've no idea where I am? Leo said nothing, but the voice had a point. *I am but a dream to you now. When you close your eyes, you can see me. But you fight me so. This is the only way that I could speak to you, to tell you that we come soon. I will not harm you, but be of an aid to you.*

He knew. In that moment he knew who he was hearing. "You're not real. Just a byproduct of me being ill. The drugs conjured you up for me and I've been dreaming of you since."

I've been with you forever. Since you drew your first breath. But the drugs did not conjure me; they only made it so that I was able to show myself to you. And once there, I never left you. But another holds me for you. When you come together, we will be as one.

The dragon in his body shifted. Or so he imagined. He'd been feeling it for days now, moving along his body as if it were real. But he knew what it was. Stress. All of them had been under a great deal of it lately, and that was all this thing was. Putting his sword back into his back, he moved to the lift and started it up. Leo decided to ignore the voice and the things that he felt. For now.

Another is coming for you. She is not happy with you living. He told the dragon that he wasn't either. So much for ignoring him, Leo thought. *You must live so that many others will as well. Should you have died, I would have been with my holder for too long and I would have burnt my host up.*

"Tell your holder or host or whatever it is that they can have you. I'm not in the mood to have any more stuff added to my body. The tats have been quite enough." The dragon laughed and told him much more was to come. "No it won't. I don't want you. Even if you're real, which I'm not saying you are, I'm pretty sure that I'd have to accept you or something before you can take me. Right?"

No. I will only need to have you touch the host and it will happen. I suppose your touch will have to be willing. I've never thought of that. But why would you not want me with you? Leo pulled the first pallet of water bottles down off the tall shelf and put it on the dock without answering the voice. He was nutty enough without being caught talking to himself. *There is nothing wrong with you mentally, Master, but you are stronger than you have shown the others.*

"How the hell would you know if you're not even a part of me?" He told him he was in his mind. "Well, that's not a good place to be for me, much less someone else. I bet you're finding all kinds of things to entertain you."

There is much there to learn about you. I have been giving you information too. You may now be able to drive the rig. Also, there is some information that I have given you on the woman that comes for you. CarolAnn Rivas. Leo wanted to tell him to stay out of his memories, but since none of this was real, it would be like telling himself not to think. *That is a good point, Master. I shall have to think on that.*

"Don't call me 'Master.' There's this being that's called that and I don't want to be...you should know this." The voice asked him what he should call him. "Leo works for me. Anything but master or anything that is similar to that."

I shall call you Leo then. Leo took two more pallets of water to the dock before he got out the hand dolly. He was pretty familiar with these too, having worked his way through college in a warehouse. *Leo, this woman that comes for you, CarolAnn Rivas, she thinks you should be dead. Her wishes are to have you dead so that she may collect on something that you promised her. But I can find no such policy in your mind.*

"Because there is none." He let his mind wander over his memories of CarolAnn. "She was to be my wife. But then I got sick and...and she decided that she'd be better off with someone that was healthier."

There is no one in her life that I can see. And she is coming here not to do you harm but to demand things. I fear that she will hurt your heart more than she has already. Leo didn't think that was possible but said nothing. *There are others in your life now. Ones that you push away, but I believe you to love. There are other ways to hurt someone than just physically or mentally.*

Leo didn't say anything again. Not that it mattered all that much, he supposed. The voice in his head was just that, a voice, and since it was right there, it could get to anything that he wanted it to. Leo thought perhaps he was having an episode. Not a good thing in someone that was set to live forever.

~~~

Jamey came out of the shelter and looked around. She had been a little disconcerted when she'd first gotten there to find the only entrance or exit was in the basement of the house. But she supposed that it made it easier to enter when there was a problem, and too many ways to get in the place would be dangerous. Stopping just before she put her weight on the foot that she'd just put on the step, she listened.

"I think there's somebody here." Another voice said that it was just leftovers, nobody was here. "No. Look. It's all fresh, like it was just put here for us to steal."

"Why would anyone put out food for us to steal, you moron? Christ. You were dropped on your head as a baby, right?" Moron took offense and cursed at the man talking. "Look. There is nobody here. We've been all over this place two times. It's abandoned, like the other houses."

Looking around the basement where she was, Jamey made sure that the door to the shelter was well hidden. Of course they might have seen it earlier, but there was no point in advertising the fact that she was living in it. Going up the stairs, she pulled out her gun and had her finger in the guard when she got to the top of the stairs. She knew that there were at least two men in the house, but was not sure if there were more.

When she entered the kitchen, she didn't see anyone. Whoever the men were, they'd taken the food and also left a mess on the floor. Jamey wasn't going to do that again, leave out food for any idiot to take. She'd been trying to be nice—older people were still trying to fend for themselves, but these guys had sounded young. Well able enough to get their own fucking food.

"Don't move." Something hard touched the back of her head, and instead of doing what the person holding it said, she turned, ducked, and put her fist hard into his groin. The gun went off above her and she had the man on the floor with her gun in his mouth and his in her other hand. He spoke to her, fear in his eyes, and she thought he said something like, "Fuck lady, where the hell did you learn that?"

"Where's the other shit?" He looked confused. "The man with you. Where is he? He was right here." She removed the gun enough for him to answer her when she had no clue what the fuck he was saying.

"Outside getting our shit. You live here?" Jamey didn't answer him but did pop him in the head with her gun. When she was sure he was out, she went to find the other guy.

He was in a big van, taking out what looked like bank bags. Laughing, she went out the door and put her gun to the back of his head much like his partner had done to her. He dropped the bag, and she could see hundred dollar bills on the top.

"You robbed a bank?" He said it was right there to take. "And what do you suppose you're going to buy with this money? You do know that there are no stores that are taking cash, no one is sending out bills, and as far as I know, there are any number of cars lining the streets for you to use. What are you going to spend this on?"

"This'll all be done soon and we'll be rich." She only shook her head. "If you don't shoot me, I'll give you a bag of it. Danny won't care. He said we got enough for five lifetimes now anyways."

"I don't need your ill-gotten gains, fucktard. But I do want you to find another house. This one is mine." He tried to turn to look at her. "Danny is in the house with a bump on his head, I'm assuming? If so, then I want you to go in there and get him or so help me, I'll set fire to your money and shoot you every time you try to go and put the flames out."

"You'd do that? Christ lady. We just wanted a home to come to. It's been hard living in a van with all these bags. And your house has some electric. There aren't many of them around here no more." She hit him firmly with the gun. "Okay, okay. Sheesh. I'll get him, but he's not going to be none too happy with this. He had his heart set on that big old bed upstairs."

"Too bad. Get him or else." Jamey snapped her fingers, hoping he'd think it was a lighter. "Get him and get out or this is gone."

He fell twice running to the house. When he came out with his partner over his shoulder, she nearly burst out laughing when she noticed that he had stuffed two of the bottles of water in his pants pockets. When he tossed Danny in the back and closed the door, she stopped him from leaving just yet.

"You return here, even to see if I've moved on, I will cut your dick off and serve it to you on a nice platter." He nodded. "You make sure that Danny knows that too. I'm not one to fuck with. I have ways and means that will make you suffer for so long you'll beg me for death."

"We're gone." He looked around the street. "Can we move in over there? We won't bother you, and we don't have any more gas to be going around finding other digs."

"No. Find another car to drive. Drive as far from here as you can and don't look back." He nodded, reminding her of one of those stupid pet tricks. He was still nodding when he got in the van and drove off. As it sputtered and jerked around, she thought they were as dumb as they came. Stealing a car that didn't run worth shit because of the cool racing stripes down the side of it was about up to par with these two, she just knew it.

Jamey cleaned up the mess. Not too much…there was water here, but she didn't want to advertise that she was using the house. But there were rats—besides the two-legged kind—and they were running around like they owned the place.

After she was finished, she went to the upstairs bedroom to shower. She didn't use the one down in the shelter unless she had to, as it was on a different kind of system.

His name is Leo. I have it now. Jamey stilled in the middle of washing her hair. *He is very angry.*

"Why? Because you bother him all the time, or do you just do that to me?" He laughed and she smiled. "You do know that you're a pain in the ass, right? That my life might have been normal if you had just remained quiet instead of telling me how to do things."

You would not have survived should I have left you alone. Which, she supposed, was true. He'd been in her head when she'd been in major trouble a few times, telling her to go one way when she was going to go another. He'd also helped her learn how to pick a lock, start a car, and get the power grids up and running. *See? I have been more helpful than you wish to say. But you do know that tomorrow you go to the compound. He will not be…he will not be receptive of either of us, I think.*

"I don't care if he is of me or not." She finished washing her hair. "I know that I'll miss you terribly, but I'll be all right now."

You cannot leave us, Jamey. I have a need for you to be in my life too. She let the water stream over her face to hide the tears. *Do not cry, my heart. I will make sure that you are as safe as Leo.*

Finishing up her shower, Jamey dressed and then armed herself. She did wonder if she'd get to keep all the things she'd gained by holding onto the dragon for this Leo person, but didn't ask. Dragon more than likely would take everything from her, and she supposed that was the way it should have been.

Her day was pretty much routine. She'd gather as much food as she could in the big car she'd been using lately to make deliveries, and take them to the few places that she knew there were people hiding. She did pause outside of the big warehouse that she'd been getting water from because there seemed to be movement inside. Jamey decided that she'd come back later and take it out tomorrow to those that needed it.

Going about the rest of her day, she did go by the warehouse later and found the big lock on the gate, and was sort of pissed about it. But instead of letting it stop her, she put her hand on the lock and shoved some of the power she had into it. When it was melted, she opened the gates and moved in.

Jamey was putting the last case of water in the trunk of the car when she realized that she wasn't alone. Moving to the door, she pulled out her bow set and waited. She realized then that she should have shut the gate behind her.

"You're stealing." Turning slowly, she looked at Skylar. "You're stealing that water. I believe we've laid claim to it by putting the lock on the gate. How did you get in? And if you're the one that melted the lock, I have so much work for you."

"I'm special." She went back to her car that was sitting in the dock area. Jamey knew that the woman had followed her and short of killing her, she just let her watch. "I've been coming here for months. I take this around to shut-ins and people living in the caves."

"I see. And how long have you been doing that?" Jamey didn't answer. Not that she was hiding the fact, but because it had been so long, she no longer remembered a time when she wasn't doing it. "If I give you a key, will you not break in next time? It's the only way we can keep the malefactors out. They don't seem to know how to pick a lock."

Closing the trunk, she turned and looked at Skylar. "You know as well as I do that there is some kind of spell around this place. You lock it to keep people like me out. The malefactors, or whatever they are, can't cross over the barrier you have up." Skylar nodded. "There are nine buildings that you have the spell on. And of those nine, six of them are filled with people that aren't from around here. And I don't mean another town...I mean, not here at all."

"You're very well informed. Who told you all this?"

Jamey started for the car and was grabbed from behind. Turning, she started to fight back, but Skylar was suddenly across the building hitting the wall on the far side. Whatever had knocked her away had come from Jamey. Jamey was about halfway to her when a huge man knocked her back.

Jamey drew her sword when he did. As they danced around each other, waiting for...she supposed a first move, Skylar started laughing. The big man turned to her, and Jamey attacked. He was down on the floor with her blade at his neck just as Skylar came up to stand at his head.

"I'd prefer that you didn't remove his head. That might be the only thing that will kill him, and I've grown quite fond of the man." Jamey didn't move but watched the man as he stared at her. "He's usually very harmless if you're not trying to kill me or, in this case, defend yourself when I'm being stupid. I'm pretty sure if you let him up, he'll tell you how sorry he is."

"I will not." The man nearly roared out his denial. "She hurt you. What am I do to, let her? She tossed you around as if...how did she do that anyway?"

He bent his head and looked up at Skylar. She assured him that she was all right, and he looked back at Jamey. She hoped to Christ this wasn't Leo. If it was, she was so fucked right now.

"I won't harm you. This I promise you." Jamey didn't move. "Skylar told me that you're the woman that has been killing the malefactors with a bow and arrow. I'm assuming that you can with this blade as well?"

Instead of answering him, Jamey stood up off him. He lay there until she backed away from him, but she didn't put her sword away. When he sat up, Jamey started for her car. These two were just too much, and she was going to find other means to help the shut-ins.

"What are you?" Jamey paused for a few seconds, then continued moving. "I'm Remy. Skylar told you about me. I'm her mate. But you're not human, so what are you?"

"Host." Turning before getting into the car, she looked at the two of them. They were warriors was all she could think. He looked like someone that would carry a broadsword and cut men to ribbons without breaking a sweat. Skylar looked like she would be right there beside him. "I won't bother you again. But if you do see me, don't fucking lie to me. I'm not stupid."

"What is a host?" This was from Skylar. "I've touched you, so I know that you're not human, not wholly anyway. Will you tell me what you are?"

This time instead of answering, she let Dragon answer. He was there, always on the surface of her body, and when she bowed back and let the image of him go she couldn't see either of the two people. He was big and mean looking even if he wasn't whole or even real yet, but it was an image that she'd used before just to scare the piss out of people who were trying to harm her. Jamey knew the moment they realized that she wasn't fucking around with them. When dragon pulled back, his body filling hers as he'd done for many years, she held onto the car and watched them. She was weak as fuck right now, but they might not know that.

"I'm holding him for someone. You know him, Leo." Remy nodded. "I'm to bring him to him tomorrow. At the compound. Dragon told me that I'd not be welcome."

"Knowing Leo, I would say not. And how do you give him…Dragon?" Jamey told him she had no idea. "You're weak now. Is that what happens when he comes out to play? You are left too weak to move?"

"Just when he cannot take me over. He pulls from me, I guess. And he doesn't leave my body. Not yet at any rate." She had no idea why she was telling them this. "He's been with me for my whole life. I'm going to miss him."

"Come with us now. We'll care for you and help you with Leo." She shook her head at Skylar. "You're not leaving here like this. One of the malefactors will get you."

"They can't hurt me. And lately, they're afraid of me for some reason." She opened the car door and sat in the driver's seat. When she was sure that they weren't going to try and stop her, she started the engine. Dragon seemed to be pleased with what had gone down. It took her nearly five hours to make her deliveries because she was so weak, but Dragon was still sounding giddy with himself.

Chapter 3

Leo listened to Skylar and Remy go on and on about the dragon. He told them that he didn't give a shit, and more than once told them that he wasn't taking anything. But inside he was terrified. The dragon was real and he really was coming for him.

When he'd had enough, or in this case too much, he left them. Leo went to the yard and pulled his sword. He wasn't going to kill anything or anyone, just yet, but he was going to burn off some energy that seemed to be brimming over the top. He'd been out there for only about five minutes when the voice began to talk to him.

She showed me today. To Skylar and Remy. I'm not sure why but she did. It was a wonderful feeling to be so free. Leo said nothing. *You are not speaking to me again. You do that a great deal, have you realized that? It is most annoying. But today I feel too good to let it bother me. I will be with you on the morrow.*

"No you won't." The voice laughed. "I'm serious. I'm not going to touch the girl and you'll just have to stay with her. And so you know, there will be no trickery on your part either. I don't want you to come to me."

He was quiet for a long time. Leo had hoped that he'd leave him alone, but there was no such luck for that. When he spoke again, his voice was no longer jolly sounding but hard and pissed.

She will die should you leave me with her. Her body cannot take all of me. I will burn her up and then I shall die as well. Leo didn't want anyone to die, but he didn't ask for this so it wasn't as if it were his fault. *Do you not care that for all these years, all her life, she has held me for you? That without her, you would never be fulfilled?*

"I'm happy with the way I am right now. And if you think about it, you would see that I'm right. Having you with me, however the hell that works, will only make me stronger. And as far as I can see, being stronger isn't what is going to stop this invasion any time soon. It's what we do, not how strong we are."

You are a fool, Leo. A fool if you think that strength will not play a large part in all of this as much as what is in your mind. Leo put his sword away and started for the house. *When she comes tomorrow, she will be —*

There was tension there when the dragon stopped speaking in midsentence. Leo could feel it and asked him what was wrong. And for some reason when the dragon didn't answer him, he grew afraid. Not that he knew why, but he pulled his sword and took a stance of defense and waited.

"What is it? Tell me." Nothing. The feelings were still there, but there was sorrow there as well. Someone was hurt, and he had a feeling it was his fault. "Dragon, tell me."

She might not come to you tomorrow, my lord. I will let you know when or if to expect her. Leo asked him what happened. *You care not for the host that I'm in enough to take me from her, so I would imagine that you have no care as to what has happened*

38

to her now. I will care for her as best I can and then when she is able, we will come to you. Should you leave me with her or not, it will be up to you.

The connection, or whatever it was, was cut off. Leo felt as though a phone had been slammed down in his ear, and he dropped to his knees. There was pain there with the sorrow. And he was sure that whatever had happened would have an effect on him for the rest of his life.

Trying to reach the dragon gave him no answer. And he had no idea how or even if he could find the girl. The little he knew about her could fit in his palm, and that wasn't enough to go about the town and search for her. And asking about a large dragon would get him committed if he went that route. Standing up, Leo staggered.

~~~

"What is it?"

Leo sat in the chair and asked for a drink. Ann handed him a large glass of tea, and he drank it down despite the fact that it was sweet tea and not his usual unsweetened variety. When he emptied that glass, she refilled it two more times before he felt as if he could speak.

"I have a voice in my head." Ann nodded and got up and made him a sandwich. "Food won't cure this."

"No, but you need it. So tell me what he's said to you and maybe I can help you. And by the way, I know that he's coming. I see it." When she sat the thick roast beef sandwich in front of him and sat, she continued speaking to him. "Eat. The voice, is it a dragon?"

Nodding, he took a bite out of the sandwich. Speaking around the bite was hard, so he chewed quickly. Christ, she knew, was all he could think about.

"There's a woman too. I'm not sure what her name is other than host. I think they might have told me, but I don't know." Ann nodded. "She's supposed to come here tomorrow and give this dragon to me, but I don't want him. And now I think something happened and I don't know what to do."

"Of course you don't." She didn't sound like she was agreeing with him but more that she was disappointed in him, and he asked her about it. "You never do anything that anyone wants you to do. You're as stubborn as my grandson when he's fussing not to take a nap."

Leo wasn't sure, but he thought she'd just compared him to an infant. When she growled at him, he realized that was just what she was doing. He started to ask her why she thought he should do this when he didn't want to, but Remy came into the room.

"There's a mess. We're up." Leo stood up and moved to the door with Remy. He heard Skylar coming right behind him and waited at the door for her. When she walked by him and patted his cheek, Leo thought that it was a little too hard to be considered a pat for friendship.

Since they were working nearly all the time, Remy had come up with a plan that they'd go out in sets of three. It was difficult at times and they'd have to call in help, but Leo thought it was working better. Fresh help when you thought it was too much had saved them from losing the battle a few times.

The subdivision was nearly overrun with malefactors. There didn't seem to be any accidents or fires that he could see where they would usually congregate, but he moved in carefully. There seemed to be something going on at a house, but no one could see what it was from what he understood from Remy.

"We've been here recently." Leo nodded. "When? Do you remember? And what happened when we got here?"

"There was a power surge. And two people died due to it. There's a junction box around here somewhere." Leo pointed to the burnt out shell of a box and then looked at Remy. "You think that someone tried to get it running again?"

"I don't know." As they got closer to the house, Leo saw the bodies. There were five humans dead, and two more that were close. He just stepped over them for now. They had learned, the hard way, that they couldn't save everyone and had to work around that. Leo hated that almost as much as he did most things lately.

The malefactors were gathered in a house at the back of the circle of houses. There didn't seem to be any reason for it, but they were also weak, confused, like they were when they'd been drawn to an area to supply energy or whatever it was to something or someone that was bigger and meaner than they were. But when they entered the circle, there was nothing there but more malefactors.

"I'm going to the basement. There might be one of those machines down there." Remy told him to be careful, and Leo said he would. As he moved down the stairs, two things hit him as really strange. There was nothing down here, not a single cobweb even, and the stairs were made of metal, not wood like in most houses. The hair on the back of his neck stood up as he moved to a door that seemed to be hallowed in light.

Don't touch it. The voice, a woman's this time, had him jerking his hand back. *It's a trap. They want you to open the door and on the other side is a monster. It's a doorway to somewhere else. You'll let him cross over if you open it.*

"How do you know?" He heard her say something but wasn't sure what and asked her to repeat it. Leo listened to her tell him she'd nearly let him in earlier. That was when he realized that her voice was weak and she sounded like she was in pain. "Are you hurt?"

The laughter was bitter, almost like she was telling him he was a fucking moron. Reaching beyond the connection that he was using, he found out that not only was she hurt but she wasn't going to survive without help. He asked her where she was.

Hiding. And I'm fine. Leo moved back from the door to see the glow around it fade. *Whatever it is, it's using those creepy guys to power the light. It's a trap.*

He could see that. Standing at the bottom of the stairs, he called for Remy and Skylar. He told them what the voice had told him. Leo never thought about her talking to him until Remy asked him who she was.

"I think she's hurt. Badly." The voice told him again she was fine. "Yeah, she says she's fine. I have no way of knowing for sure, but I can connect with her on a deeper level and she's far from fine."

"Ask her if she's Jamey." He did and the voice told him to tell Skylar to fuck off. "It's her. She's mouthy and I'm going to enjoy sparring with her. Tell her we'll come and get her. Just find out where she is."

"I've asked. She said she's fine." Leo had a feeling this woman and the one that was coming to see him tomorrow were one and the same person. Skylar confirmed it. "I was talking to the dragon when he told me that she might not make it to see me tomorrow. I think this is why."

"Well, can you ask the dragon where she is?" He tried to reach the thing, but he was being just as stubborn as the woman was. He told Skylar that.

"She'd have to be, I guess. I think she's been on her own a lot longer than even this shit had been going on. And when I touched her the other day, all I got from her was that she wasn't human. I can't read her, nor can I figure out just what she is. Host is all we know." Leo moved up the stairs when they did. Remy spread his wings and told them he'd be back, and he left him and Skylar there. "Leo, why don't you want the dragon? Aside from it being something we've never encountered before, I think it would be amazing to have him as part of me."

"I have enough." He didn't elaborate, but she asked him again. "Look, I think I've made it clear that I didn't want this shit either. And now that I have it, I'd like to be at the level I am now. It's a lot of stuff and every day I'm figuring out more. I just can't think that having a dragon would make that much difference."

"It will to her."

Leo nodded and didn't say anything more about it. When Remy returned with several sticks of dynamite, Leo started to the other houses. If he blew this house and there were humans in any of the other houses, they'd be killed too. But no one was in the homes and there didn't seem to be any lighted doorways to the other realm in any of them either. As Remy set up the explosion, he and Skylar went door to door again to gather what they could use at the compound.

Most of the time they only checked for drugs, the prescription kind along with as many over the counter things as they could get their hands on. Not that they were running low, but they didn't have anyone in the group that knew how to make more. Weston Page, their in house doctor, knew the compounds for them, but he'd never made them. So they took what they could.

They were just coming out of the last house when Remy came out of the basement of the first house. He'd checked that house too because he had a pillow case full of something when he came out. Leo was lifted from the ground by Remy just as the house exploded. The fire around it was burning the house on either side when they felt the power of the hit touch them.

By the time they were back at the compound, Leo had tried to reach the woman and the dragon several times with no luck. Christ, this was all his fault and he had no idea if he wanted to fix it or not.

~~~

Jamey wasn't touched by the group of malefactors around the building she was supposed to go to. Which was good because there was no way that she'd be able to engage with any of them, even if they gave her a head start. She was weak with the wound that had nearly killed her.

The doorway had been in her home, in the lower level that her shelter was in. She'd never seen it before, and what had scared her the most was the fact that when she'd come out of the shelter, everything that had been just outside the doorway had disappeared. Not even a single box had marred the basement floor when she noticed the doorway.

Ever cautious, she moved to the door slowly. Dragon had been quiet for some time, and she figured that if there was going to be a problem, he'd let her know. As she started to touch the door, the handle almost calling for her to do so, she heard something or someone up in the kitchen. Malefactors had gotten in.

There were perhaps fifty of them. They were milling about the house and yard like they didn't have a clue about what the fuck they were there for. Some of the ones in the house had fallen down, their bodies seemingly spent, like they'd been sucked dry. Going into the yard, she could see that there were a few that were having the same problem, like there was a drain on them and it was near where she was. Going to the basement again, she looked at the door and had that feeling again that if she didn't open the door and soon, she was going to die from it.

Jamey walked around the basement several times before she finally went to the door. As soon as she touched the wood surrounding the handle, she knew that she'd made a huge mistake. The power—the dark magic—that hit her threw her across the room, slamming her into the wall. The things that had been in the basement appeared just as the door started to open.

Jamey pulled her bow and arrows out. As she made her way to the door, she fired arrows into the frame as quickly as she could let them go. Whatever was on the other side started screaming then, was cursing at her and telling her to stop. Just as she got to the door, the wood covered with arrows, a hand—really a claw—came out of the small opening. Jamey pulled an arrow out and stabbed it into the creature, and fell against the door to slam it shut when the long nails disappeared back into the light.

Within seconds, the door faded out and the things in the basement reappeared. Jamey felt herself tumble forward and knew that she'd really hurt herself somehow. It wasn't until the dragon told her to get up that she found the strength to not just stand up but to stagger her way to the shelter and lock herself in. She had landed on something, and it had pierced her body. Taking out the large chunk of wood had made her bleed profusely, but it was her head that hurt the worst. And she felt like she was on fire all the time.

And today she was going to deliver her savior to a man she didn't know.

He'll not take me on. Dragon sounded so sad that she paused before stepping over the circle that surrounded the house. *Do you know what will happen to you should he not?*

"Yes. I'll die." She thought maybe she was close to that now but said nothing. "Is that why I'm hot? Not like a fever, but hot like I'm boiling?"

Yes. I'm close to him. He is near and we both know that it is time for me to balance you. You will be all right, my heart. As soon as he touches you. You must make him touch you. Jamey wasn't going to do any such thing. If he didn't want her friend, then she didn't want him to have him. *You will die. I do not wish for that to happen.*

Taking the last two steps over the magic, Jamey felt her breath catch. There was a great deal of it here, magic. Different than what she'd found at the doorway, but here it was a clean feeling almost. This was pure magic and felt good to her. Almost like she could bathe in it and feel better than she had in years.

But with the clean feel of the magic, her wound felt like it was opening again. She'd tried to patch herself up, keep the wound from bleeding, but it was too big, and she'd lost too much blood. Staggering once, she felt herself fall forward and wanted to lay there. But someone touched her and Jamey looked up.

The little boy startled her. She'd expected people here, yes, but not a child. When he smiled at her, she rolled to her back and looked up at him. He sat beside her and asked her if she wanted him to go and get help.

"Yes, please. Leo. I have something for him." The little boy nodded but didn't move. "I don't have a lot of time here. Could you hurry?"

"I've called for my dad. He's coming."

Jamey closed her eyes and must have drifted some. A man asking her if she was able to move had her looking up again.

"My name is Hector. You must be Jamey." She nodded. "They're out on a mission right now. Even Leo. But I'm going to pick you up and take you to the clinic. Can I touch you?"

"I'm hot." He nodded, but when he touched her she had to smile at the look on his face. "The dragon said he was burning me up. I'm to let Leo have him before that happens. But he doesn't want him."

"I'll see to that." Jamey closed her eyes again when he put his arms under her body. But the pain was overwhelming and she cried out and reached for her sword. "Please don't, young Jamey. I cannot help you should you take off my head."

"Hurts." He told her that he could see that but she must lower her weapon. "Yes. I'll do that."

It took what seemed forever before she could get her arms to do what she needed them to do. The sword seemed to slip from her fingers just as she got her arms to lower. The little boy told her that he had it and would care for it for her. She told him to put it near her, that she might need it.

Wave after wave of pain took her away only to bring her back again and again. She saw a man standing over her and knew that he was some sort of doctor. There was a woman there as well, but she had no clue who she was and faded out again before she could form the question to ask. Dragon was there as well.

Please, my heart, let me go. If you do, then you will live. It's not worth it. She told him no, screamed it at him to just stay with her for a bit longer. He argued with her. Someone else did as well, a woman who she was pretty sure was Skylar.

Jamey felt as if she were in a furnace. Not like a hot sun was beating down on her, but that the sun was inside of her, burning its way through her. She supposed on some level that was right. The dragon was becoming too much for her.

Let me go. She turned away from the voice in her head, her dragon. Letting him go without the man taking him would kill him, she knew. If not both of them. When someone touched her, she knew a new kind of fear and tried to pull away.

"Give him to me." She cried out when he told her again. His voice wasn't like her dragon but louder, angry. "Give him to me. You said he was mine. Now fucking let me have him."

The pain was incredible. She felt her body bow up from it, nearly bend her in half. Heat, hotter than before, settled over her. Her entire body hurt worse than ever before. Screaming out, begging for death, she heard the man tell her to let go, and when she could fight it no longer, the dragon left her.

A peace settled over her. No more pain to take her breaths away. Her body cooled down, and she could feel her heart beating again, normally, not like it was powering a freight train. When she felt herself being lowered to the bed, Jamey opened her eyes and looked at the dragon who stood by her, and put out her hand to touch him. When he pulled back, she felt a new kind of pain in his rejection.

"I've taken him, but I want nothing more to do with you." The man was Leo, she supposed, his voice harsh and full of hatred. "You'll live and I'll have this thing that you had in me forever. Thank you very much."

Jamey let her exhaustion take her. But she knew that as soon as she woke—if she did—she'd leave this place. Wherever it was. And mourn the loss of her friend to a man so cold and so cruel that she knew that Dragon would forever be lost to her.

Chapter 4

Leo didn't take a turn sitting with the woman. He had had enough of her, and as far as he was concerned, the sooner she was out of his life the better. But that didn't stop the others from giving him updates about her until he'd finally told them that he didn't care. That had been four days ago.

He supposed he should have been happy that they'd done what he asked. But he wondered about her. And the dragon, to be honest. He'd not spoken to him once since he'd taken him from the woman, and even that had been done with not a word from him in the changing. And Christ, when he thought of that moment when he saw him come from her body, Leo shivered.

He'd told her to let him go, to let the dragon come to him. She'd fought him, nearly with her last breath. But when her body was almost spent, she'd not been able to hold him any longer. Leo figured had she been healthy or not injured, he'd still be telling her to let the dragon go.

The lights had started at her fingertips. He'd reached for her hand when she'd put it out, and as soon as he'd touched her, he felt all of her pain. Not just that, but everything about her had come to him with that touch. By then he'd not been able to think beyond what was happening to the two of them; to do much more than try to run screaming from the room.

Her body had risen from the bed; he thought the dragon was fighting as much as the woman. But when he pulled from her chest, his body lifting out of her as if she were a shell, the dragon looked at him with eyes as green as the grass. Leo started to back from them, but the dragon leapt at him, his body knocking him back and to the floor just as the woman lowered to the table, her body resting as if she were dead.

There was no time for him to check because the dragon moved into his body like he was taking him over. Bones broke; his skin burned away. His body shifted beneath his skin and muscles screamed to stretch to accommodate this new thing. Leo screamed then, the pain taking his breath away until he fell to the floor, his mind shutting down. It was the most painful thing he'd ever felt, and he was sure that it had hurt the woman more than it had him. By a long measure.

When he stood near the sink in his kitchenette, he felt it move under his hands, and that was when he figured out that he was taller, bigger than before. Leo had hated the changes that he'd had no control over, but he could see where it was going to be helpful to him. His rooms were different too…not that he'd thought about it at first, but now his bed was larger to fit his new body. His dressers were taller, his shower was wider. Leo had gone to Weston to see what had changed.

"You're six inches taller and about sixty to seventy pounds heavier. Not fat, but all muscle. I would guess it was the dragon." Nodding, he let Weston take his blood pressure and listen to his heart. "Your heart rate is faster, but I would guess that's about right with the change in your species. And your blood pressure is lower. By a great deal."

"I'm hungrier too." Weston nodded and told him it was because he was hotter. "How much hotter am I?"

"Your temp is about one sixty. I'd say that's normal for you. When Jamey was dying, her temp was about 210. You've come down a little since you took on the dragon, but not much." He didn't ask about her, and Weston didn't tell him. "I'd say that you should eat more and drink a lot. I don't know shit about what you are or how this is going to affect you, but I'd like to see you daily to keep a log if you don't mind."

He told him he'd be back, and he had been. The temp had stayed the same, his blood pressure and other vitals had been alike, and his appetite had finally leveled out. He told Weston just that morning that he was burning about ten thousand calories a day. Ann had told him that she'd keep more protein and red meat in the house for him. Some days he found himself wanting to eat it right out of the package. But he'd not done that. So far.

Now he was lying on his couch. The television was muted and something was there, but he wasn't focused on it. All he could think about was that he had a dragon inside of him that was silent. Leo knew that he was there because he could feel him move, but he never talked to him.

The knock at his door was almost welcoming, and he got up to see who it was. Leo had been resting for the last few days. They had been going out on runs, but he'd been left behind for some reason. He supposed it was because he was still slightly weak from the dragon.

Vicki was standing at the door when he opened it. She stood there for several seconds before she spoke.

"She's gone." As she turned away, it occurred to him who was gone and he called her back. "What is it you want now, Leo? To know where she went? I don't know. How did she get out of here? I have no clue. When Weston went to check on her, she was gone. No note, no anything. Remy asked me to tell you. I did. Now I want to go back to Davis and have him hold me."

"How long has she been gone?" Vicki shrugged and didn't say anything. "You know, you've been treating me like I'm the bad guy, and I didn't even want to come here. Much less have a dragon put in me."

"Then leave." He felt his heart twist in his chest at the venom in her words. "Get out. Leave. You work hard like the rest of us, but to be frank, I'm sick to fucking death of hearing how you've been bought here against your will. How this dragon has changed your life. You never once asked how it affected us, did you? Or how it was for that woman to lose something from her that had been there her entire life. Did you know that? That he's been in her body, just waiting for you to take him from her, for nearly thirty years? How it has been for her doing this for you?"

He never said a word to her when she turned and left him. Closing the door behind himself, he sat on the couch again and stared out the window. Christ, they all hated him and it was fucking not right.

"Will she die?" The dragon stirred under his skin but didn't answer him. "Will she die? Will not having you in her body keep her as safe as it was before?"

She will not die from me not being a part of her. That was neither encouraging, nor was it terribly helpful. *She is my other half, as she is yours. A balance of things to come. You know this as well.*

"What do you mean she's your other half?" No answer, but then he really hadn't expected one. "I will not have her in my life. I have had my heart ripped from me before, and I'm in no mood to take on another woman just to satisfy some perverse sense of balance in the world."

Then you must only do what you have been doing up until now. Leo asked him what that was. *Nothing.*

Leo left his little apartment in the compound and went into the yard. He was pissed and he could feel the heat of his anger running all over him. The dragon tat—he supposed it was really a sigil—moved along his back to his chest. Leo tore off his shirt and watched it move. That was when he saw it for the first time. Not the dragon itself but the woman there that was in his claws. The dragon held her still.

"You're keeping her there with you even though you'd have me believe that she is gone." The dragon opened his hand, and Leo looked at her. "She's...what's wrong with her?"

I told you, my lord. She is not going to die by my not being with her. But I must keep a part of her with me should you need me. Without her, there is no me. Without me there is no you either. Leo asked him to explain. *I know not how to. Only to say that the two of you create me. Without both, I am not a single. I have no balance.*

The dragon was telling him that without the girl, he would never shift. And Leo had a feeling that should he need the dragon, for anything, the girl would die because she was already weak and not here with him. He asked the dragon where she was.

Below the earth. I know not where other than she is buried beneath it in a house. Leo tried to think what he meant. *A shelter, she called it once when she was fighting with men who would kill her.*

"Someone is trying to kill her?" Dragon told him that someone would always try to kill what it did not understand. "Do you know where the house is? The shelter might be something that is…a bomb shelter."

The house is not far from here. She walked here the day that she gave me to you. Leo had heard that she'd walked, not driven, to them despite the wound that had nearly killed her. *You should be able to touch her mind. She is in both ours.*

Leo reached out to her—Jamey, he knew her name was—and felt her. "She's in pain. A great deal of it. But resting the best she can. Why did she leave here if she wasn't healed?"

Because her task for us was finished. Leo went to the garage. He couldn't fly like the others and wasn't going to use the dragon, even though he figured he could. But he had a feeling it would end her life before he found her. *I can see where she is. Sort of. It's a cul de sac. She's living where there is power and other houses that are occupied. The house is…it's on a circle street lined with trees and…Dennison Street. The house is on Dennison Street.*

He drove like a man possessed. Leo had no idea why, but there was an urgency inside of him that made him reckless and drive much too fast. Twice the dragon told him to slow, that she'd be there when they arrived, but he needed…needed something right now. Pulling onto the street, he knew just where she was. The house was surrounded by more malefactors than he'd seen in a while.

"What's wrong with them?" The dragon had no answer. "They look…color? Is that color I see?"

I do not know what they looked like before. Perhaps you could give me a moment. Leo felt him touch his mind. It was a gentle touch, but he felt it all the same. *Yes. These beings are much different than the others. I believe they are feeding from her power.*

"Power?" Again the dragon had no answer for him. Getting out of the truck, he went to the house. Unlike the other malefactors, these didn't try to attack him. In fact, they avoided him completely, going so far as to open a path for him to the house. When he entered the house, Leo made his way to the basement to find her.

Looking around the neat basement, he totally expected to see the woman's body lying there with her heart stopped beating and her breaths no more. He reached for Remy and told him what he'd found and why he was there.

I'm going to bring her back with me. I'm not sure...I don't even know what sort of shape she was in before she left. He felt stupid for not knowing a thing about the woman other than her name was Jamey and that she'd given him more than he'd wanted.

Serious to bad. Weston said he'd like to have kept her a couple more days, but she said her job was done and she needed to get to her shut-ins. I'm guessing she means the people she's been helping out that are hiding from the malefactors. Skylar said she thought she'd been doing it for a while now.

He remembered someone saying something about that before. How the woman had been helping others out at a great risk to herself. He moved to the large door on the other side of the room.

It was a shelter like he'd thought it was, he'd bet his life on it. But he had no idea how to open it, and even if he did know how, whether she'd meet him at the door with a gun or not. He'd only had contact with her once, and she'd been in so much pain, he doubted that she'd remember much about it. Smiling, he knocked hard on the door using his fist.

She is coming to the door. I have spoken to her. Leo thanked the dragon when he spoke and waited. *She will not be able to converse with you long, I'm afraid. She is weak and getting more so all the time.*

"She's coming back with me to the compound. Do you think you can help me convince her to do that?" The dragon said nothing. Leo heard the door locks being disengaged and he stepped back. What he didn't expect, and more than likely should have, was seeing her standing there with an arrow pointed at him. And Leo had no doubt whatsoever that she'd use it on him if he made a wrong move.

"I'm here to take you back to the compound." She didn't move, but he could almost feel what it was costing her to stand there. "I'm going to come inside, all right? The dragon said that he spoke to you. I won't harm you, Jamey."

"I've done my part." Her voice was low, but he had no trouble hearing her as he made his way to her. "You should just get the fuck out of here before that thing comes back."

"What thing would that be?" She told him about something coming through a portal and let the bow down to hold onto the table just inside the door. Leo grabbed her just before she fell and lifted her into his arms. Closing the door behind him with his foot, he heard the locks engage and was grateful for one thing going right today. "I'm going to lay you down. Can you point to your bedroom?"

She was out, her body hanging limply in his arms. Leo made his way through what looked like a smallish kitchen through the living room and found the room he was looking for. He could smell her in this room. Her weakness and blood, both old and new, permeated the room.

Laying her on the big bed, he stepped back and looked around. There had to be a medical kit here somewhere, and when he found it, he went back to her. She hadn't moved, not even to straighten her arm out that had fallen from the bed. He put it across her chest and then picked it back up to see the markings.

"You've been marked to match me, it looks like." He studied the markings that ran from her shoulder to her wrist. They were the same as his, but hers were bloodied and he wiped at them before looking at the wound in her right shoulder.

"I'm going to cut your clothing away from you. I don't want to have to move you around to see to your wounds." He took out the scissors and started at the sleeve of her shirt. "I've never had to undress a woman like this. Usually, they're naked before me."

He flushed and told her he was sorry. To talk about his sex-capades with a woman while she was hurt was just cruel. Leo tried to think of something else to talk about rather than think about what he was doing.

"I've been such a bastard. Not that I won't continue to be one, but I've been better than usual. There's this woman...well, cunt is a better name for her, but she's ruined me for other women." He got the sleeve cut to the neck and then started at the bottom of the tee she had on. "I'd been sick you see, dying actually. And then this man came to see me and he healed me. I didn't ask for that to happen. I was ready to die."

"Too bad." He stilled in cutting away her pants when she spoke. Leo looked up at her and into the greenest eyes he'd ever seen. "People get shit on all the time and you can't think you're any better. Or do you think that you should have things better because you're so good looking?"

"No. But she told me that she wasn't cut out to be with a sick man. Other things too, but that was what stuck in my mind most of all." Jamey snorted at him. "I was dying and she left me because it would have dragged her down."

"Better to have found out then than to have married her and found out later." Jamey lifted her head and looked down at his handy work. "You're paying for this. And I'd really like to know what the hell you're doing taking my clothing off anyway."

All kinds of things popped into his head. Making love to her. Just to taste her a bit. And to drink from her. His teeth shifted in his mouth and he knew that somewhere along the line he'd been given fangs. And the need to sink them into her creamy flesh made them ache.

"I've come here to see how you are." She didn't say anything nor did she stop him when he started to pull her shirt open. "I'd heard that you were hurt so I came to see how badly."

"What do you care?" He had no answer for her but looked down at the wound that was nearly as long and as wide as her entire shoulder. "There was a blast at the doorway on the other side of town. Much like the doorway that was here. But by the time I got there, he was about through. The others had rigged up some dynamite and blew a hole in the wall. I don't think anything came through, but I have no way of knowing. A monster was trying to come in here the other day, but I hit it with my…I shot the door full of arrows and it kept coming. Then I stabbed him with an arrow and he left. Taking the door with him."

She rolled to her side after yawning, telling him that he could lock up when he left. Leo only stared at her, trying to think about everything that she'd just told him. Leo relayed the information to Remy before turning Jamey around to face him again.

"What the fuck are you doing now?" He told her that she was going with him. "Oh no I'm not. I'm not sure what you think you're doing here or even how you got in here, but you have my dragon. Now get the fuck out —"

"I can't use him without you." Her mouth snapped shut audibly. "Yeah, I thought so too. But he said that we have to balance each other. That you have to be a part of him as much as I am."

"He told me that I only had to give you to him. I have to admit that I thought that all my stuff would go with him and was thrilled to shit that I still have it." He asked her what. "The bow and quiver. Also the sword. I did...what are you shaking your head about?"

"You have a bow and arrow on your body? And a sword that you...you can peel these things from your body?" She nodded and Leo stood up and pulled his shirt off. Turning his back to her, he asked her if it looked like his.

"No. Mine is here, on my hip. The quiver is on my back and yes, there seems to be an endless supply of arrows. But I had that long before I came to you. Years." He nodded and asked her if she had a dragon now too. "No, not really. Just a part of him. I think perhaps I was never meant to hold the entire thing."

"That's not what I said. I asked you if you had one now." She stood up and he reached for her when she staggered. Her body fell against his and Leo felt his cock thicken and stretch. She must have felt it too, because she looked up at him.

"I'm not having sex with you." Her voice was husky and warm sounding, and Leo found that he wanted to hear her screaming out in that same low voice. "You're insane if you think that I'm going to go to bed with you when you already told me that you wanted nothing to do with me."

"I've not changed my mind, but I want to fuck you. I won't, but I want to." She nodded and backed away. The dragon stirred beneath his skin and when she stopped moving, he wondered if she could feel it as well. "What is it?"

"He told me that…the dragon said that we're in danger." Leo looked at the door, then at her again. "Not with the malefactors, but with each other if we don't balance him out."

"How?" She told him she had no idea. But the need to touch her, feel her body next to his, had him halving the distance between them. "Christ, I want you. Like I've never wanted a woman before."

"Get over yourself. We're not having sex." But she didn't move when he was close enough to feel her breath on his face. "I'm not kidding you. We're not having sex. Not now, and not ever."

"Let me kiss you. Perhaps that's all I need." Her head was shaking even as her tongue moved along her lips, making them moist just for him. "A kiss. Just a single kiss."

Leo only touched his lips to hers. The taste, even as brief as it was, made him want more. Need more. When she moaned, Leo started to take her mouth again, her body molded against his. Leo wanted to tumble her into the bed again and take her. Just as he was trying to think how he could do that and not hurt her again, a loud voice told him to take cover. Leo pulled her down with him as the wall behind them started to tumble things atop them both. Leo was sure that something had blown the shelter up and that they'd be buried alive down here forever.

Chapter 5

Master had never felt this good in his life. He had been made thousands of years ago, of course, but even then after the conversion of his old body to this one, he'd never felt like he could have taken on the world and won. Randall came into the room as he did everything. Fast and without thought to what he might be interrupting.

"I have a man that says that he can duplicate the drugs we're taking. So I brought him here to work with the shit we have. But there's something wrong with him. Come tell me how to fix him." Master got up and moved to follow the other man.

Master had taken the best house in the realm as soon as it was established that they would need to stay here for little while, and that house just happened to be Ward's. It would have been so much better had it been Dolin's, but that house had been destroyed along with nearly a city block around it. He supposed now that he should have taken better care, but he'd been mad and didn't think well when he was angry. Master was still trying to figure out how to get into the door that he'd found on his last visit there. Dolin had a shelter, and he was in there with Ward. He just knew it.

As they walked to the lab, Master asked him what the man had told him. "Nothing yet. There's something wrong with him. And so you know, yeah, I did go down to the other place to get him and bring him back. He can and does make the best shit ever."

"Shit?" Randall nodded to him. But before he could ask him what that meant, he entered the room where the chemist was laying. "Oh my. You didn't say that he was human."

"What does that have to do with stuff? He can mix anything up and give you a high." Master moved closer to the bed and could see what it had cost the young man to come to this realm. He had been...most of him had been left behind was the only thing he could think of. "Why is he breathing like that?"

"I would think that a part of his lungs have been left somewhere in the space between here and there. Should you have brought him over nearly dead, then none of this would have happened." Master touched the side of the man's face where it was whole, ignoring the part where more of it was missing than not. "You would be better off killing him now, ending his suffering so that we don't have to look at his body for long. Consult me the next time you have a person brought here."

Master started to leave the room when Randall grabbed him by the arm. "You can't just kill him off. He's a friend of mine. I promised him gold and riches for making this shit for us."

"I do not believe he will be capable of doing much more than just lying there for the next few days. If that long. Perhaps, as I have said, if you had consulted me on this matter, then he would be around to make your *shit*." Master decided that whatever this shit stuff was, he wanted no part of it. "That man is as good as dead now. Part of his body, including his brain, is missing. His left leg is nearly gone, and he is losing blood faster than he came make it. You have killed him just as if you put a bullet to his head. And perhaps that would have been better. Now he is nothing."

Master left the room as Randall shifted. His anger was profound if the wreckage sounding in the other room was any indication. Smiling to himself, Master made his way back to his house and then decided to go to Dolin's house again. The camera there that hung above the house was just too much temptation not to have fun with.

Master was extremely disappointed that they could not get anyone to help them with this project. When Ward and Dolin had been in charge, there had seemed to be many chemists around that were working nonstop on getting formulas made up for them. Not that he knew anything about what they'd been doing, but they had been plentiful in their efforts. Now there was no one there. Not just workers, but there wasn't a soul around anywhere. Even the animals that had been plentiful were nowhere to be seen.

The house that he'd been going to came into view, and Master stood watching it. There was something off about the thing, and it took him several moments to figure out what it was. Someone had been straightening up the area. There were neat piles of trash and paper stacked up in one area of the yard. Wood splitters were in another. There was even a pile of clothing that was so muddy and ruined that Master had to laugh. But now it was being cleaned up.

Walking around the camera so that he wasn't in the view, Master looked at the different things. He had an idea that someone was looking for something, but what he didn't have a single clue. There was a pile of papers, not the newspaper kind but what looked to him like things that had been in the lab. Upon closer inspection, he realized that they were indeed from the lab...the logo was blazed over the top. It was the only thing he could make out.

Master picked these up. He had no idea how to read other than to recognize his name, and it was there several times on the pages. *Benton,* it said in typed letters, so he rolled them up and stuck them into his pockets to take to Randall. He might have been mentioned there as well, but he had no way of knowing.

Frowning, he realized something else. The little plot that had been made for Mary had been cleaned up as well. The bench that sat in the flowers was sitting up now and there were fresh cut flowers on the little stone. Careful of the camera, he walked there.

"You should have seen them when you died." He had liked Mary and thought her to be the smartest of all three of them. It had been her that had been the kindest to him, and he would never forget that. "Now I have to work with Randall and he is a moron. Much like I think Dolin and Ward are. Did you know that all the people here are dead? Everyone but them. Well, not Randall and I, but the rest are gone. We might have never been here but for the houses and stuff."

He looked around again and wondered what someone had been looking for. He moved to each pile, looking and kicking at the things there, but nothing seemed to come to him. As he made his way back to the area, he turned and looked again at the piles. That was when it occurred to him.

"They're coming up here. They are stuck there in that shelter, and now they are coming above ground." Of course that was obvious, but for him it was like a light had gone off. Yes, they were moving things around, but they were coming up here to do so. They were leaving their little hidey hole, which meant that he could find them here.

Dancing a little jig, he wandered away again without taunting the camera. He wanted them out, and now that he knew they were about, he could stay hidden until he caught them. It mattered little to him which one of them was coming above ground; he'd have them both soon enough.

Going back to Ward's home, he nearly missed the man coming out of his house. There he was. Ward. Ward was walking to the cart that hadn't been there before and putting things into it. It looked to be clothing and a few items that seemed to be heavy. Master watched him as he made his way back into the house, presumably for another load.

Master wasn't sure what to do. He could kill the man. There was no one about to help Ward should he try to run. Besides, Master was much stronger than the puny man and could take him out without even shifting to his beast. But it would take some of the fun out of it.

If he didn't kill him right away, he could take him to the door of the hidey hole and make him have Dolin open the door, but he didn't want to be closed into the little area, because he had no doubt that it was small with the two of them there. Even if he managed to kill them, then there was the chance that he could be stuck there too. That wasn't going to work.

He'd have to have a plan. A good one. One where not only was he the victor, but they also knew that he was. Master was sick to death of anyone thinking that he was less than he was. Master knew that he was far superior to anyone that had ever been born. And that included Remy.

That was something else that had been bothering him a great deal. All the things he'd said to Remy hadn't given him the satisfaction that he'd hoped for. And where had Remy gotten his information? No one that had been there when Remy's family died was still alive...they weren't even around on the day after to tell Remy what they had done. Or what he hadn't done. Where had he gotten the truth of what happened that day from?

Then there was the white magic. He'd had Randall look it up the other day, trying to find what he could about the white power that had come from the strange woman who had hurt him. All it had told him was that she was more than likely a powerful witch or something like that. Randall had gotten bored with helping him and had only given him part of what had been said, he was sure of it. There were many more words on the page than just witch.

He'd been hurting so badly that he'd thought himself close to dying that day. And he would have but for the drugs that Randall had given him. And now...it seemed that the drugs that had kept them healthy were running low. Or so Randall had told him the other day. The utopia had been and still was the best part of the day when he got his daily shot. But just this morning he'd been told that his dosage was going to be cut in half.

"Why mine?" Randall told him that since he'd gone to all the trouble to get them, then he shouldn't have to be suffering without them. "That does not seem all that fair. I should think that since I'm the one that has trained you, I should get as much as you."

"That's not going to happen. Just be glad that I'm giving you any at all. And in the event that we don't find someone to brew us up another batch, we're going to be hurting soon anyway." Randall had walked away from him laughing. Master had made it his work to go through the entire lab, as well as Randall's house, looking for the drugs. They were somewhere and Master wanted to control who got what.

Going back to the house after he watched Ward gather another load and then leave, he thought of a plan. It had to be perfect, and it was going to be his. Randall would not be told what it was, nor that he'd seen the man. Then he thought of something.

Master was going to keep them both, Ward and Dolin, alive for a while to make more of the drugs. They'd know how to do it, and then Master would destroy them. It would be his greatest pleasure.

~~~

Jamey opened her eyes and started to panic. It was dark; not a single speck of light was coming from anywhere around them. Trying to move the weight off her body, she heard Leo moan and wondered how badly he was hurt, because she knew that he'd taken most of the beating when the bomb or whatever it had been went off.

"Just give me a minute." She told him he was heavy and he laughed. "It's not all me that's on you, but a wall I think. Or a book shelf. Why don't you have one of those fancy readers instead of all these books? It wouldn't have hurt so badly when it fell on me."

"They were here when I got here. And in the event you forgot, there is no Internet here, as well as very little in the way of books to download should I have one of those fancy readers." When he shifted above her, Jamey moaned. "I think my leg is stuck under something else besides you. It feels all twisted up."

"Let me look. Hang on a second." She felt him move again and thought maybe she'd tell him to lie still when he was gone. His weight had been heavy, yes, but without it she felt...deprived of something. His hand searched along her body until he got to her breast, and she moaned with him when he cupped it. "Christ, what I wouldn't give to see you naked right now."

"It's not going to happen." He laughed, and she slapped his hand away. She sat up and could see a pinpoint of light that she knew was coming from the kitchen area, so she cleared the debris from her leg, then stood and made her way there, being careful where she stepped. "There's a generator in the kitchen. Give me a second and I'll get it turned on."

He might have said something, but she didn't care. The sooner he was gone the better. But when he put his hands on her shoulders as she reached for the generator button, Jamey screamed. He moved her out of the way before she could see what he was going to do.

"The generator might have been damaged too. I'm just going to test it in case it might blow up." Good plan, she thought, but said nothing. Instead, she started picking up the chairs that had been dumped over as well as a few things that she could see from the small blinking light from the room where Leo was working.

She made her way into the room where they had been, and while it was dark still, she could finally make things out. The bookshelf had indeed fallen over, and the books that had been on it were all over the floor. Jamey had just sat it up and was putting the books on the shelves when the lights flickered on. The hum of the generator was still going when Leo came into the room with her.

"We need to figure out what happened above us and see if we can get out." Nodding, she continued to pick up the books until she realized how exhausted she was. Her body was spent so when she sat down, he was in front of her in seconds. "How badly do you hurt?"

"I'm fine. I'll go to bed again after you leave." He shook his head. "I'm fine. I don't need you to do anything else. I appreciate you fixing the generator, and when I get rested, I'll go up and see what the damage is."

"I'm not leaving you here. I can smell gas and that's more than likely what happened." Jamey only shrugged and leaned back on the chair. She felt the dragon stir but said nothing to Leo. "You can feel him too, can't you?"

"He was supposed to leave me." Leo said nothing as she closed her eyes. "When I got back here, more than likely before that, the mark on me had changed somehow. It's a dragon, but not like it was before. Only the quiver and other weapons were whole, but now he is as well."

"May I see it?" She stood up and turned her back to him. He'd been all over her body, the dragon had, but she knew where he was at all times. It was as if he were— "I don't think he left you so much as separated into two parts so that we each have some of him. I think that we're supposed to be together before he'll come out and help us."

"No. I don't believe that. Besides, I don't want any more to do with you than you do with me. And sex with you doesn't count as us being together. It's just been a while since I've been in the mood, and you caught me with my guard down." He lifted her shirt, and she knew that he could see him. When the dragon moved, Jamey tried to keep herself from tensing up when Leo put his hands on her. "Maybe some of him got left behind."

"Turn around." She did as he said and took a step back, nearly falling in the chair when she noticed that he had his shirt off. "I think if we come together we'll bring him out. I'd like to see if touching our dragons together makes him stronger."

Jamey wanted to find out, but there wasn't any way that was going to happen. But before she could tell him to go fuck off, she was being dragged to the doorway and out into what had been a nice orderly basement.

"Christ." She could not have agreed more with Leo. "What the fuck do you suppose happened here? If this was a gas explosion, and I'm really thinking that's what it was, then it must have been a main line. Because there is nothing left that I can see."

As they climbed out of the hole, she could smell gas stronger as they made their way to the top. And once there, she wanted to go back down and hide out in her shelter rather than see what she was seeing. It had been an explosion, a huge one too if the area around them was any indication. Everything on the cul de sac was gone.

There had been five houses in the circle, hers being the first one and the one across from her where the street met around the boulevard. Even the trees that had been there, some of them as high as forty feet, were nothing but rubble, and the road a rock garden around it. Along with the others, her house was leveled in the blast.

"We'll have to contact someone to come and get us." If Leo had come in a car, there was no evidence of it. Not even a tire mark was around them. "Jamey, you can't stay here. There is a gas leak and until it's taken care of, you can only assume that it's going to blow again."

"There were people in some of these houses." He nodded but said nothing. "I have to see if anyone survived."

"No one did. I can smell death and blood. And unless they had a shelter like you did, there was no way that they could have survived that blast. It leveled everything within a few blocks." Jamey turned away from him. It was not like she knew any of the people, but they had been alive until this thing happened. "Remy and Skylar are coming to get us. They heard the blast at the compound and are glad that we're all right."

"I'll have to start all over." Walking to where the shelter had been buried, she looked down. "Had any of the lines been into the shelter or even close to it, I would have been killed."

"Whoever built this thing knew what they were doing." She had thought so too. It was really too bad that they hadn't been able to get to it when all this began. "Remy wants to know if you are afraid of heights."

"No." She had no idea why that was important but didn't ask. She was trying to think where she could go now that was as safe as where she'd been living when she saw Skylar standing in front of her. "There was an explosion."

"Yes. We heard it. Are you all right?" Jamey nodded, then shook her head. "I think that's about right. You're not bleeding and I think that the blood on your shoulder is from something before this happened."

"Yeah, I was fighting with a something that was coming through a wall after me and I had to shove it back. I got knocked on my ass for my troubles. I thought it was because of the dragon, but now I don't know anymore." She was babbling, and she was pretty sure that Skylar knew it. "I'll need to find another place to stay. I don't know where yet, but I guess it won't be here."

"No. Not here." Jamey looked around again and saw Remy talking to Leo. Neither of them looked all that happy. "Leo said that we're to take you to the compound, and Remy said that he can't make you do anything. I think you should come with us as well, but I won't force you into anything. I think you could hurt me if I tried."

Jamey sat down. Her body just seemed to give up on her and her knees turned to jelly. When she was being lifted up, she looked at Leo and tried to tell him she was just tired. But he told her to shut up.

"You're very rude, has anyone ever told you that before?" He told her many had. "Well, you are. Put me down. I just need to rest. It's been a hard day and I've been through a lot in the last few days. You being the worst part of it."

"You're going to the compound if I have to tie you up and take you there in a wagon." For some reason that struck her as funny and she laughed. "This is not fucking funny. With you there it's going to be hard not to have sex with you."

Jamey heard the sharp intake of breath and knew that it was Skylar. If she was close enough to hear him then so was Remy. Struggling to get down, Jamey nearly knocked Leo down too when she got away from him. When he reached for her again, she staggered back into a hard body and knew it was Remy.

"I wouldn't have sex with you if you were the last man on earth. There are toys I could use that would be warmer than I think you would be." His anger seemed to lash out at her, yet he said nothing. "You are a mother fucking prick and I wish to Christ I had never met your ass. You're a...you're a...oh my God, I'm going to fall."

The ground was coming up fast. She could see something shiny in the dirt just as her vision blurred, and realized it was a dime. Then there was nothing at all.

Chapter 6

Dragon knew that they were both together. He could feel it as if it was a fine meal, and he was set to sup on it. The host was weak but getting stronger now that she was near her mate. Soon they would come together and he'd be stronger for it as well. When he felt the male, Remy, coming closer, he reached out to the man with his newfound strength, and it surprised them both when Remy staggered slightly from the touch.

You are lord here? The man told him he was not. *I believe you to be wrong about that, sire. You are much stronger than any of the others, but you rule them with a fine hand. Leo, my master, he respects you more than he does anyone else.*

Be that as it may, I am only the man who started this, not the one in charge. We work as a team on all things here. And we make decisions as one as well. Dragon knew that about the man. But Remy did not realize that his word and his ideas were weighted heavier than the others. *What happens with you and Leo now? Do you know what it is you're going to add to our group?*

I am a dragon. He knew the lordship was struggling with things and what they could do. Dragon was sorry that he had no more information to give him than he knew now. *I can help you should Leo need me, but I know not what I can lend to you and the others in way of information. I am...I have been in the dark, as you call it, for many years.*

Are you large? Or the same size as Leo? Do you breathe fire? Should we give you more space when you are out of him, or do you – ?

Out of him? His lordship explained. *I am not a separate part of Leo, but him and his mate. We are one. When he needs me, they will form me. We need to have a balance. A balance that is three.*

I don't understand. Neither did Dragon, and he told him as much. *What do you mean, they form you? Do you understand that enough to explain it to me?*

We are a single body, at least for now, but it will take the three of us. Without them, I would not exist. My host, Jamey, has held me in safe keeping for her entire life. And that of her foremothers as well. We have – me and my hosts, the women that have carried me – been waiting for the male to come to us that would make me whole. He didn't think he was explaining this well at all, but the man seemed to understand.

You're saying that for generations someone in Jamey's family has been waiting for Leo to be born so that you could be a part of their lives? The man entered the room where Leo was. Leo had long since fallen asleep, his body at rest deeply because dragon had commanded him to be. The same with Jamey. They needed to rest, and they would not on their own. *You're very old then.*

I am ancient. Older than you by tens of thousands of years. Remy sat in the chair as he nodded. *You are old as well. Older than the people who are here save one. And he is nearly as old as me.*

Hector. He's from another realm. Dragon knew that. *Can you speak to me face to face or can we only talk through this link?*

I can pull from the body, but it will harm them because they are so very weak. I should like to have them rested for when they come together. Remy told him that it didn't look like the two of them were going to work things out. *They will need to. For too many years I have awaited him. Now that I am a part of him, I cannot wait for another generation to take me.*

You'll die. Dragon nodded. *Why did it take so long for you to find Leo? Or did you even know who he was?*

Every generation there has been a male, a being that would take me from my host. One that would take me unto him and bring me forth. Each time when he was close, I could feel him. Over oceans I could feel his need to come to the woman, to be my master. Dragon felt the sadness of it consume him. *Every time there was an accident. The male would fall ill, something would kill him while making his way to us. And through it all the woman would love none like she would him. But for a time she would find some happiness. She would live out her days until a child would be born to her. Then that girl would hold me to her when her sire would die. It has been...a very long time since I have been freed.*

You've been out before. Dragon told him when he was but a hatchling, his mother, a ruler of their kind, had put him into her handmaiden to keep him safe when others came to kill her. *I'm sorry for that. But this thing with the two of them, Leo and Jamey. What will happen to them should they not come together? Leo has been hurt badly, and I don't think he'll come to this easily.*

Remy told him the story, or what he knew of it, and said. *She is on her way here, Leo said. He said that when she arrives he won't talk to her. I think that's about as big as mistake as he can make. I've been around a long time and I don't think women — determined women like this one sounds to be — can be put off so easily.*

You are right. But this woman has hatred in her heart, and has since before she came to be with Leo. She wants only one thing, and that is money. This person feels that he slighted her because he did not die when he said that he would. Remy laughed, and Dragon joined him. *I have tracked her to nearly here. CarolAnn Rivas...she travels not alone, but with men that are set to come to see you as well. CarolAnn will arrive within a couple of days with a man that seeks to murder you as well.*

Ward or Dolin? Dragon told him that it was neither of them but a monster that had been here before. *Benton. His name is...was Augustus Hill. He was...not really a friend of mine, but we were on the same battlefield when I was changed. I think he was as well, but not into anything that was helpful. Now he calls himself Master, but they know him as Benton. He's partly responsible for the death of my wife and children.*

I have no way of tracking him all the time. Just glimpses of him. He is...he is lost to me when his mind is functioning at a rate that I cannot see. And I think him to be somewhere that is not of this realm. I do believe that he is with the other man, brother of one who lives here as well...he is with that man. Remy told him his name. *Randall Carver is a man that is unwell in the head. And he is full of drugs that make him hard to keep in my mind. Benton as well. They are both using a manufactured drug that has enhanced their body but eats at their mind.*

Do you know if it's things from this realm or from the one that Hector is from? He told him both. *I see. They were using agates when they first came here. Using them to make some of the people that we fight stronger. Some of them were even able to speak. But we've been collecting them when we find them, and I think that their supply is now exhausted. At least I hope so.* Dragon told him he had no idea about that. *Neither do we. We've only just begun to make a list of the things we can do. Each of us carries something unique to each other, and when the mate comes, it enhances it greatly. I can do things that some of the others can't do, and them me. We could write a book on the things that we do not know. It is…it is most vexing to me, as my mate would have me say.*

I can tell you that the markings on your body are old. Older than even me. They are from a race that is thought to be dead, but they are not. There are not many of them, but the few that are living are stronger than their counterparts ever were. I can no longer remember what they were called, but I will give it some thought. Remy told him he'd appreciate it. *It might do you no good, but at one time I knew where one of them was. I will have to wait until we are whole before I search for her. She is…this woman can be very nasty when she thinks that others will want more than she wants to give them. I have only met her the one time, and it was enough. My host was most displeased with her use of magic. I think she bore the scar of it for more years than most would have.*

Remy stood up, and Dragon stretched out. Leo was waking despite the fact that he should be resting for a bit longer. When he stood up as well, Remy told him that they had been talking.

"He has decided not to speak to me. I think I've pissed him off." Dragon could have pointed out that he could hear him but was pretty sure that Leo knew it. "He is under the misunderstanding that I should have sex with Jamey so that he can be whole, whatever the fuck that means."

"I think it means that you're not listening if you don't get that. I guess…you know what, never mind. You will do as you please anyway." Remy moved to the door, and Dragon wanted to call him back. He had enjoyed talking to him. But he turned and spoke to Leo before quitting the room. "If you don't come together, all of you will die. I don't know that you'll suffer much, but none of you can live now without the other. Perhaps you should let him explain it to you rather than barking that you're not going to come together with your mate."

"I don't bark." Leo must have realized that was just what he was doing because he told Remy he was sorry. "I have no heart left to let her into. I have given all I can to someone else, and she tossed it back at me. And to let her into the shell that I have would be unfair to her and me. I don't want a woman in my life."

"Then I feel sorry for you." Remy left them then, and Leo moved to the window. Dragon wanted to be free so that he could go out and spread his wings, but he knew that it wasn't possible just yet. Dragon did wonder if he could trick Leo into being with the woman, and decided to try that. There could be no more strife between the couple than there already was. He made his way to Jamey to bring heat to her body. It was all he knew how to do.

~~~

Her body was hot. Not just hot, but it felt as if she were being stroked with a hot flame. When Jamey opened her eyes, she sat up in the bed and realized that while she was alone, she could feel the presence of someone else. She was pretty sure it was Leo.

Moving her legs on the bed to get up, Jamey moaned. It was as if she were close to coming. Moving again, pressing her thighs together, she felt her clit burn with need and reached her fingers down to her pussy to stroke herself. The need that was there, the heat billowing from her, was enough to make her bow up off the bed as soon as she touched her fingers to her wet pussy.

Cupping her breast while she played, she thought of Leo when he'd tried to kiss her. His mouth had been hot, even for the brief time he'd been touching her. And his cock was thick, full, and long. Her fingers moved faster along her nether lips as her juices flooded her hand. Christ, she was so close that she knew when she came, it was going to be epic. But the sharp knock at the door had her moaning in a different way, and she told the person to go away. The door opened anyway. It was Leo.

"I came to talk…what's wrong with you?" Her face heated more, and she pulled her sheet away from her overly sensitive body. Even the sheet was too much and she wanted him gone so that she could finish herself off. "Are you sick? I can call the doctor if you want."

"No. I want you to get the hell out of here." He, of course, did the exact opposite and moved toward her. "Go away, Leo. I'm not in the mood for your shit right now."

"You're aroused. I can smell you." He sounded as shocked as she felt. But when he jerked the sheet off her, she realized that she'd left her gown up and he could see her. He stared at her pussy for so long that she felt herself getting wetter and started to pull the gown down to cover herself when he grabbed her wrist. "Don't. Show me what you're doing. I want to watch you."

His voice was deep, deeper than it had been before. Jamey wanted to beg him to speak again, to command her to masturbate while he watched again, but he let go of her arm and told her again he wanted to watch.

Sliding her fingers down her body, she moved them between her legs and spread them wider so that she could show him. Then, with her eyes closed, she slid her fingers between her wet lips and touched her clit, imagining his tongue there, his fingers doing what she was doing to herself, feeling her wetness soak her hand. He said her name and she looked up, her mouth watering as she saw him standing near her with his cock in his hand.

"Come for me. Come and let me taste your pussy while I jerk off." Her body was so close to doing just what he wanted that when he leaned over her and licked her clit, she came hard, her free hand holding him to her as she fucked herself faster with her fingers. When he sucked her clit into his mouth and bit down, Jamey cried out again, this time begging him to take her.

He sucked at her pussy, bringing her three times before he lifted his head. His eyes were dark and she could see fangs as they curled below his lower lip. Jamey felt her own mouth shift until she was sure that she too had them, and the need to bite him was making her reckless.

"Take me. Now. Bite me while you take me." Leo nodded, climbing up on the bed even as he fisted his cock. She wanted to taste him as he had her, but only wrapped her fingers around him as he sat on his knees between her legs. "Fuck me. Please. I need to feel you fuck me."

Not saying a word to her, he moved up her body. Small pains of his bites took her breath way and she wanted more of him, all of him. When his cock was at her entrance, she felt him fill her with his crown before pulling out again. She pulled his head up by his hair and looked at him.

"This changes nothing."

Her heart twisted in her chest just as he slammed forward. Every part of her body felt his possession of her. Her mind seemed to shut down when he touched her as deeply as he could. He started to pound her, taking her so hard that she knew that when he finished, she was going to be sore. But when he nuzzled her neck, licked at her flesh, every part of her pussy and body seemed to be on the verge of something huge. When he told her to come, commanded her to do so, she let go. The climax screamed from her just as he sank his teeth into her throat. His cum filled her hotly;

his body continued to fuck her even as she felt herself falling again over a long deep cliff.

Jamey pulled his wrist to her mouth. Licking the pounding pulse there, she bit him too and tasted his blood as it filled her mouth. She thought of all the times she'd had sex before and knew that this was different. Not just the biting, but everything about it. And she also knew that despite what he said about it changing nothing, everything was different now. There would never be any going back from this.

His body was covered in a fine mist. Wrapping her other hand around his shoulder, she held him to her as she drank from him, their eyes locked as if it were a battle to be won. When he threw back his head, his entire body stiff with his second climax. Jamey sealed the wounds at his wrist and came with him. Nothing could have prepared her for the emotional climax that she had as well.

She was complete. There was no other word for how she felt when he dropped his body atop hers but that she felt as if she were whole. Leo didn't speak to her, for which she was grateful, and she thought instead about what they had just done. It wasn't making love but a fucking, she told herself. And now they were one. Turning her head from his face when he lifted his head, she expected him to say something, but he only rolled to his back, leaving her there to feel alone.

"We shouldn't have done this." Again she said nothing. What could she say? "The dragon put you up to this, didn't he?"

"He lives within your body now, not mine. And if you remember correctly, I told you to go away." Leo chuckled and she ignored him by rolling to her side away from him.

"I'd very much like for you to get out of here. I'd like to be alone."

"I never loved her. I thought I did, but I didn't. When she said she'd marry me I was more disappointed than I was glad for it. There was no one left in my family and I thought that it was time for me to get married. Maybe have a child or two of my own. But about two weeks later, I fell at work." Jamey didn't want to hear about his life with this other woman, but he continued before she could tell him to get out again. "I'd been tired a lot. Stress, I kept telling myself. It was test time again and the kids weren't working the way I'd hoped they should. Not that it mattered in the long run, I guess, but most of them were going to fail and I'd be fired."

"Standardized testing?" He told her yes. She wanted him gone so said nothing more, asked him nothing else. More than just from her room, but from all of her life. As much as she knew that it was going to be impossible now, it hurt her that he cared so very little about her.

"I was in the hospital for three days before the doctor came in to talk to me. He suggested that CarolAnn come in too, but she had a hair appointment that just couldn't be missed." Jamey turned to look at him to see if he was being serious. But he seemed to be lost in the telling of his story and didn't look at her. "I'd already figured out that it was going to be bad news. Really bad news. Cancer, I just knew it was cancer. So when he told me I had a rare form of leukemia, it wasn't really a surprise. CarolAnn came in later smelling of hair spray and something only hair dressers know what it is, but she made me sick and I started to throw up. It had been the first meal I'd had in days that day, and I was a little pissy to her about it. Of course, she was shitty to me in return. I didn't deserve it, but there you have it all the same."

"She was shitty? Well, too fucking bad for her." Leo looked at her then and asked her what she meant. "You were just told you were going to die and she was shitty to you. What kind of person does that to someone that is sick?"

"She meant well, I suppose." He lay there for several seconds, then shook his head. "No, she didn't. CarolAnn had her own set of standards for what would go and wouldn't go with her lifestyle. And I just wasn't it when I got sick. I suppose, like me, she was settling. But for me it wasn't as if I would have left her when she got sick. She couldn't get away from me quick enough."

"Did you know what kind of person she was before you asked her to marry you?" Leo shrugged. "I don't understand. Did you or didn't you?"

"I did. I suppose in a way I was settling, like I said. But that doesn't mean that I didn't think we could make it work. I was hoping that we could." Jamey snorted at him. "I was alone and she filled the hole that I had."

Jamey got out of the bed and pulled on her clothing. She only had one set of things here and would have to go by the shelter to get more before moving on. There was no way she could stay here with this idiot. To think that she was going to settle too. He leaned up on his arm and watched her as he continued.

"After I was let go with all kinds of meds and rules, she moved in with me. I had no idea why she did it until about three days later when her friends started coming by. They were there to see her sickly future husband." Jamey paused in pulling on her boot to watch him. "I wasn't looking much different yet. I'd been healthy, or pretty much so, up until I found out I was dying, and some of them were disappointed that I wasn't bed ridden. They said that to me. Anyway, after things started to fall apart for me, throwing up the meds and anything I ate, losing weight, stuff that comes with dying I guess, they stopped coming around. And CarolAnn was having a hard time...she called it 'dealing with me.' I wasn't fun any longer. I was keeping her from the clubs and worse yet, I could no longer go out into public with her because I was so tired all the time."

"She wanted to show you off. How she was living with you to care for you and you weren't cooperating with her plan." He told her that was pretty much it. "But you still were going to marry her."

"No. I'd already figured I was never going to be her husband. I have no idea why, but...when she gave me back the ring, I was relieved. But then she told me that she needed my social security number as well as the name of the insurance company I had the policy with. I asked her what policy. And by this time I'd been out of work for about a month. No money for insurance policies by then, of course, and if not for the health insurance that I had, I'd have been out on my ass as well." Jamey was still trying to wrap her head around the gall of this bitch when Leo lay back on the bed and continued. "She said that since my mother had finally died and that I had no one else, that she would collect my insurance when I was dead. She even told me that if I really loved her that I'd just die now and she'd get the money sooner rather than later. So I explained to her that there was no money coming her way. In fact the house we were living in was a rental and I was behind in the rent now, so she would lose that too. I wasn't, but by then I just didn't give a shit. My heart had had enough of her. But she thought she'd be out sooner rather than later. CarolAnn kept insisting that I had a life insurance policy…that everyone had one…and that I was being cruel to her teasing her about it."

Leo got up then and pulled his pants on without any underpants. She felt her body respond to the fact that he was bare beneath his jeans, and when he turned to her, she thought he knew what she was thinking, because when he pulled his cock free, he was hard as a rock as he walked to her.

"I'd very much like for you to lean over that chair and let me pound you from behind." Her entire body wanted her to do just that, but she only stared at him as he got closer to her. "Will you lick me then? Suck on my cock until I come down your throat?"

"Yes." But before she could get a taste of him, even to touch him, someone pounded on the door behind her. "Fuck."

"Leo, Jamey, we have to go. Now." Remy pounded on the door again before telling them they were rolling in five. Jamey looked up at Leo as he stared at her.

"I'm not going to fall in love with you. I'd like for you to stay here, at least long enough for me to figure this dragon out." She nodded, not even sure why she'd done that. "I'd like to have you in my room too. Please?"

"No. I'll find a place to stay here, but I'm not living with you. And while I'll fuck you too, you'll not kiss me." He asked her why not. "Because it's a sign of respect for the other person, and I don't respect you any more than you do me. Plus, it's a sign of intimacy that we don't have." He told her okay and left her to go to his room. Jamey had a feeling she'd just made the biggest mistake of her life in this, and hoped that she wasn't going to lose her heart to this man. But she had a fear it was nearly too late for that too.

Chapter 7

Dolin was going to murder Ward. Every day he was going out and leaving the door unlocked. And every day he'd have to explain to him why he had to lock up behind himself. Today, however, had really pissed him off. The nerve of the man telling him he was being selfish.

"What do you mean, I can't bring this in here? You're just being mean to me just because this is your house. Don't be selfish, Dolin. It's very unbecoming. They're my things." Dolin looked around the small area that they were sharing and wondered how long Ward had been bringing things in here before he'd found out about it. "You have your things. And I don't even think you got that clothing in here for me. I do believe that it's your cast-offs."

"Of course it's my cast-offs. I never planned for you to be here when I had to come down here. My things are all over the place here because this place belongs to *me*. I let you live here to keep you safe and because we loved Mary, but I never thought you'd be so…so…you're a slob, Ward. However did you live without a wife to clean up after you?" Ward puffed up but didn't say anything. "I don't have the room for you to bring your things down here. Whatever happened to your house? Has it been destroyed as mine has?"

"No." He flushed then. Ward had a ruddy color anyway and flushing made him look sickly. "But I'd like to have some things of mine, Dolin. I'm living here and I have to have some things of mine. Things that Mary gave me."

Dolin just walked away. He was sick of this and while they'd not seen Benton in the cameras for several days, he was pretty sure that the man was still up there. Dolin started to turn and ask Ward if he'd brought the stone, the one that he'd been finding on his person for weeks now, but didn't. It was bad enough he had to admit to himself that he thought that Mary's ghost was doing this to him. The magical stone had been destroyed…burned, hidden away, and even thrown into the lake. Yet it always appeared again. It was enough to make a man mad.

Two days ago the stone had shown up sitting by a picture of the three of them, Mary, him, and Ward, when they'd gone on a trip together. Then the next day, after he'd planted it on Ward when he left the shelter, it had shown up in Dolin's bathroom with an earring that evening. He was pretty sure it had been Mary's too.

Today had been the killer though. He'd found it in the bottom of his tea cup. As he drank the last of the brew in the cup, the stone had hit him in the lips and nearly had him screaming. Tossing both the cup and the rest of the tea into the rubbish, he sat in the kitchen for an hour staring at the stone. He knew it was going to move, just knew it. But it did nothing but sit there taunting him. When he wrapped the stone in a towel and tossed it out in the dirt as Ward had left, he realized that the cup had been the one that Mary had used when she'd come to his home for a visit.

Dolin was sitting in the office when Ward came in and sat across from him. "I'm sorry. I've been a real ass and I'm very grateful that you've let me stay here. I'll try harder to follow your rules."

"I'm sorry as well. We've been down here for a while now and I'm feeling the pinch of being cooped up. I'll be glad when this is over too." He stretched out and looked at the picture across the room, and closed his eyes before he panicked. "Ward? Are you...have you seen your stone?"

"Yes." Dolin looked at him when his voice sounded so afraid. "It's in a new place every day. I think...I think we have a ghost."

"Me too. Mary?" Ward nodded and pulled the stone from his pocket. "I've thrown it away. Buried it. I've even put it in the rubbish bin that we burn every day. And it shows up. With things that Mary might have used or that were hers."

"It's why I've been going out as well. To try and rid myself of it. I've started to bleed again as well. I think...why would she be doing this to us?" Dolin said he had no idea. "Do you suppose she's making us suffer because we've done nothing to avenge her death? It's all I've been able to think about. We should go and kill Rembrandt so that she'll leave us in peace."

"Do you really think that's it?" Ward nodded. "To be honest, I've been trying to think why she'd be doing this to us too. And that's it. I think...yes, I know that's it. Good job. We'll start making plans now."

He pulled out a sheet of paper and nearly screamed when the stone was sitting atop his desk blotter. The blotter was the one that Mary had given him so many years ago for his birthday. Ward got up and came around the desk and stared at it as well. Neither of them said a word as Dolin scooped it up with the paper and put it across the room.

"We have to hurry." Dolin nodded. "She's not happy with us. I still don't know why they had to kill her. It wasn't right of them. Not right at all. We had done nothing to them other than to try and kill them. But we were well within our rights as superior beings. They should have known this and complied."

"I don't think they understand the rules of the game. I truly don't. They go about killing our creations as if they have all the rights in the world. Should we do that, then that would be all right, of course." He lifted his hand when Ward started to speak. "Yes, I know that we have been sort of responsible for killing a few of their kind, but it wasn't us. It was the creatures. They did the killing, not us."

The laughter nearly made his bladder let go. He knew that laugh. Dolin had heard it a great many times over the decades he'd worked with Hector. Dolin was glad that Ward had not gone back to the other side of the desk and was beside him when Hector suddenly appeared in the room with them.

"You two are the stupidest men I know. And believe me when I tell you, I've been searching for dumber men." Dolin started to tell him that they were not stupid when Hector cut him off. "Shut the fuck up and sit down. It's my turn to talk and yours to listen."

Ward actually sat down on the floor. Dolin helped him up and watched him as he pulled up the chair he'd been sitting in and sat down. Hector moved about the room slowly, seemingly walking through the furniture around the room.

"You're not here." Dolin looked at Ward when he spoke. "How are you using that the other way around?

Show us how to do that. There are places that I'd like to see to...."

"Show you how to do this? Are you fucking insane? I wouldn't show you how to save yourself should you be in a dire situation. You murdered my wife. Why on earth would I do a thing—?"

"You left us no choice in that matter, Hector. We were going to murder you too once we learned how to do all the things you'd invented. But murdering your wife was needed to make you cooperate with us. Or so we hoped. But you messed that up as well. That is most unkind of you." Hector sat down on something that wasn't in their realm. Ward continued talking as if it didn't bother him that the man was sitting on air. "Where have you been staying? It's very unfair of you to not let us know. It's very hard for us to find you to finish the job without knowing where you are. I have a plan, but it would not hurt me in anyway should you tell me where you are."

"You have a plan? What sort of plan?" Ward nodded and looked at Dolin as Hector laughed. "I'm all ears to hear what sort of plan you have for me."

"We need you to help us out by killing Rembrandt and the others. Soon, as a matter of fact. They've been messing with our...did you know that they killed our Mary?" Hector said that he'd been there when he'd done it. "Shameful thing to do, Hector. You should have saved her for us."

"Like you did my wife?" Dolin waved him off. It wasn't the same thing. Not even close. "What is this plan you have for me and what do I get out of it?"

"You get nothing out of it, Hector." Dolin looked at Ward as if he didn't understand Hector, but continued before he could figure it out. "I need for you to have the spell taken from the compound that you're living in. All of them, if there is anything else preventing us from going in and having those people killed. If you help us, then I'll have the malefactors kill you quickly and before we have them kill your son. We know that he's alive, you see. Mary told us."

"So I take down the barriers and let you in...you're going to kill us all?" Dolin told him that they'd be here but they'd send someone do to it for them. "I see. So you don't want to actually do the deed but want me to help with it. Then what will you do, once all of us are dead? I'm sure you have a plan for that as well."

"We do." Dolin was actually thrilled to have Hector cooperating so readily. It was like when he'd been working in the labs with them again. "The earth will be scoured for all the stones we can find. We have a few buyers that are still interested and then there will be more once they find out what we have to offer. The world there will no longer need them and we can be rich from selling them. Also, we're going to move into the nicer homes and set up our own world. There is no one left here to rule over, and that isn't any fun, now is it?"

"And the others that are left...the humans that haven't been killed or changed. What do you plan to do with them?" Dolin didn't know and said as much. "You should also be aware that there is no one left here because they've followed us to the new realm. They've been working for us. For a good wage. I never realized how many people you two pressured into jobs that were not what they were suited to."

"They're there? On the realm you're on?" Hector nodded and smiled. "Oh Hector, that isn't right. Tell them to come back here this minute. We're having to do for ourselves and there is no one to pick up the rubbish bins that are at the end of the streets. Did you know that the stores have been all boarded up? No one...tell them to come here this minute and we'll let their punishment be at a minimum. It should be harsher the way that they've left us in a...how could they do that to us?"

"I'm sure that if you asked any of them, they'd tell you it was because you two are fucking nuts." Dolin stood up and was told to sit down. "If you get up again, I'll come there and cut your heads off. I'm in charge of this meeting, not you."

"You're being most rude, Hector. Rude to the point of making me upset." Hector stared at him for several seconds before he laughed. Dolin had no idea how to handle this person that Hector had suddenly turned into. His level of meanness was something he had no idea how to deal with. And Ward looked just as confused.

"You two have been so much fun, but now that is about to come to an end." Hector laughed again before he continued. "We're stronger now than we were before. The books that were brought to me, my books, have gone a long way in treating some of the less severe malefactors touches. And as for you killing off the people in the compound? Well, that's not going to happen either. I'm not going to help you, and I'm sure that no one there will either, should you ever get to talk to one of them. Did you know that all of your power sources have been destroyed? It was really dumb of you to think that we'd not take care of them once we found them."

"Those were ours. You had no right." Ward started to stand and apparently thought better of it. "You fix them right now, Hector, or I shall have to send Benton back down there to get you."

"Benton is still alive?"

Ward looked at Dolin when he looked in his direction. Was he? They had no idea really other than the few times they'd seen him in the cameras. But it had been days since he'd made an appearance, so who knew? "I would have thought that the last time he was on our realm that he'd have crawled into a hole and died by now. What of Randall? What is his progress?"

"He is most uncooperative. Why, you should see the lab after he left there last week. Killed off all the lab workers that we had there, and took all the medications that we were using to enhance him to take over for Benton. And I've never met a man that would complain about the dumbest things. He said that the clock was too loud." Ward smacked him on the leg, and he glared at him before continuing to tell Hector what the man had put them through. "So far as we know, he is dead too. Or we hope so. He is the most...a great deal like you at the moment. Very rude and not helping at all. I don't know why we thought he'd be a good candidate to come there and kill you. I suppose that it has to do with his sister being a part of the party that you— what is it, Ward?"

"You're telling him everything." Dolin looked at Hector, then back at Ward, who was nodding. "He'll know all our plans now."

"And I thank you for that." Hector stood up and stretched. "I'd like to say that it's been a pleasure, but it never was talking to the two of you. But I will leave you with this. The stones are not being brought to you by magic or by Mary, but by me. And every time you think you've destroyed it, it's me bringing it back to you. And I will continue to do so until you're both so eaten up with the poison of them that I will piss on your rotting corpse. Oh, and I'd be careful what I drink from now on too. Slipping a little blood into your food and water won't be that hard, after all."

Dolin sat there for hours after Hector left them. Ward said he was going out and that he'd lock the door, but Dolin didn't comment. All his mind could focus on was that Hector was trying to kill them. There was no reason for it that he could think of.

He'd killed his wife, of course, but they had killed their Mary. It was even so far as he could see. Actually, Dolin and Ward had lost the most. Mary had meant a great deal to him and Ward, and there had been no purpose in killing her as far as Dolin could see. And now that Hector had his books back...how had he even gotten them? Dolin got up to look for the stash.

They were still there, the six books. None of them made any sense, but he still tried to study them. There were words that he could understand, of course, simple words, but there were too many that were not right that made him think...perhaps these were not the real thing. Could someone have substituted these for the books that Hector had actually written? Dolin could not figure out why everyone was mistreating them. What had they done to deserve this treatment?

Hank had been in charge of the books. And when they'd raided his home weeks before he...he had disappeared. His son had as well. Then they had turned up on the other realm, and...he had the books. Dolin just knew that was the case. Dolin got up to pace.

"Hector said he has the books. These are obvious fakes." He glared at the books in question. "No wonder I couldn't read them. Someone is going to pay for that. And now he's trying to kill us. Why?"

"Why indeed." Dolin turned so quickly that he nearly fell over. Randall was sitting in the chair that had been occupied by Ward not long ago. "Hello, Dolin. Whatcha doing?"

"How did you get in here?" Dolin yelled for Ward and wasn't really surprised to see him being brought in by Benton. "What is the meaning of this? You're not supposed to be able to get in here. Get out now and lock the door behind you."

When Benton told him to sit down and shut up, the second time someone had told him to do that today, he let his temper show. Benton laughed at him and then did the most horrific thing he'd ever witnessed. He tore Ward's head off and tossed it onto Dolin's desk. Dolin fell back, his mind shutting off.

~~~

Leo watched Jamey as she fought beside them. He knew that he'd hurt her somehow, but he thought that being honest with her was better than letting her think that anything was going to happen between them. Of course, he was hurt by the no kissing rule, but would abide by it for her. For now anyway. Soon she'd want it as badly as he did.

He sliced his sword through two more of the malefactors and then took the head off them both before moving deeper into the fray. There weren't as many as there had been, of course, but there were a great many of them. Leo killed two more when he felt the air around him stir and his dragon pull at his body.

Release me. Leo asked him how he was supposed to do that. *I am not sure how, but you must. I can help here with the monsters. There are many of them yet to come.*

Leo moved toward Jamey and asked her where she was marked. She told him that she'd been marked for a long time and that she was sort of busy right now. And why the hell did he want to know now?

"Remy and Skylar only have to touch their marks together and this blast comes out of them." Just as he said that, the two he'd been talking about came together, and bright magic poured from their fingertips. "Davis and Vicki can do that same thing. If you're marked in some way, perhaps that would be the way for us to bring out the dragon inside of me."

Jamey moved toward him. When she put out her arm, he noticed that it was bloodied and wondered if she had been marked today again. Lifting his arms to hers, he waited for something, anything to happen before he had to move to take out a few more of the malefactors. He told the dragon he was open to any and all suggestions.

You have lain with her. You are one. I do not know why you cannot summon me to come out. In the event you have not noticed, I have very little to go on as well. Neither did he, but Leo didn't have time for question and answer time as a horde of more malefactors came toward them.

He'd noticed recently that they had gotten more...he supposed aggressive would have been a good term. They were faster too. He'd also noticed that several of them had learned to drive cars, and motorcycles as well. Even the faded ones, the ones that had been easy to kill, had picked up the ability to speak. There were other things as well. Things that were small on the whole but when put with the rest, it was showing them that they were fighting a losing battle.

"What if you just said, come out and help me." He looked over at Davis, who was covered in malefactor blood. "You know, sort of like '*open sesame*' or something like that. Just tell it to come out and get the fuck busy."

Leo was willing to try anything. He was exhausted and he hurt. Plus he wanted to sit down with Remy and talk to him about the rule that Jamey had put on him. No kissing? How insane was that? He was fucking her, for Christ's sake.

"Dragon, come out of me and help." He felt stupid but tried again. "Will you please come out and help us kill these things before we get hurt because we're so tired?"

He looked at Remy when he stood in front of him. Remy was protecting him while he figured this out, but he had no idea how to get the dragon to get his ass in gear. He turned his back to the man and helped clear a path to the larger group of them when the dragon spoke to him again.

You are not balanced. Leo asked him what that meant and, of course, there was no answer. But he did think about it, and all the other things that the dragon had said to him. Balance, as in they had to be together. Well, they were. But were they touching right now? No. He made his way to Jamey again to see if she had any ideas. When she glared at him, he wanted to kiss her right then.

"The dragon said that we're not balanced." When she answered him, her voice stringing together words that he'd rarely heard, he had an idea that the dragon heard her when he laughed. "I'm pretty sure that's not going to be possible for either of us. I have no idea what he looks like, and I'm pretty sure that I cannot bend over that far. But what do you think he means?"

"I fucking don't care. He's your dragon." One of the malefactors knocked her into his arms and he begged the dragon to help. Apparently that was all he needed, because in the next second he felt the dragon move.

Leo held onto Jamey as his body seemed to come apart...not like he was being dismembered, but more like he was changing. And as he watched her face, he was pretty sure that Jamey was feeling it as well.

There wasn't any pain, but he knew that he had to hold onto Jamey or there would be. When she gripped his shoulders, Leo knew that any second they were both going to be...he thought they'd be different. When his body was consumed, just literally pulled into a vortex, he let it go. Fighting would have been futile anyway.

"Holy mother of Christ." He looked at Remy when he spoke and fell back. Leo noticed that he looked odd, out of shape and smaller. That was when Leo realized that he wasn't the same size. His body, along with Jamey's, was now dragon-sized, and he felt powerful. Looking at the sea of malefactors, he knew the moment they saw him. As they started to run, Leo and Jamey went after them.

"Don't let me go." Leo told Jamey that he had her. "What's happening to us? Why is everything out of whack?"

"We're a dragon. We're our dragon." The malefactors seemed to disappear as he raked his hand over them. It wasn't like they just died but they burned up, disintegrated into nothing as soon as he touched them. When he realized that he had no control over his left arm, he asked Jamey to try it. When she moved his arm, he finally got it. They had to be balanced. They had to control the beast inside of them.

They worked for over an hour just putting their clawed hands out and raking them across the monsters. Trees and buildings were destroyed as well, because they weren't used to the size of their bodies. They just hoped that no one would come back and make them pay for this. But the malefactors were gone now, and in their place was a pile of dismembered bodies as well as their blood.

Leo wondered how they were to become human again and decided that he really didn't care. This felt wonderful.

Chapter 8

Dragon felt amazing. His body was free for the first time and he was helping his masters. As soon as they touched and told him to help, he knew that was what was needed. The way he could be free. Dragon was finally able to work his magic as he'd been born to do.

Touching his hand to the monsters, he moved through the crowd, killing as many as he could, careful of the things that were not harming them. He only just barely managed not to bring a building down on the others. He was a dragon and the earth was his home.

Swiping his large claws through the throng, he saw them disappear, much like his ladyship had done with her arrows. Dragon knew that he'd done that as well. Given her something to keep her and those that she cared for safe. He would protect them both with his life if it came to that.

Blood stained the earth. He mourned the loss of its life, but the monsters were plentiful and they were killing the humans. Dragon knew that it would be centuries before the ground would be ready to receive new life. Sad as that was, he knew that it was a necessity in these times. He worked hard, keeping his body shielded against the things that would crawl to his heart.

When there were no more monsters to kill or destroy, he looked around at the bodies. Moving toward them, he was careful to only touch the ones that were dead, and keep his body and breath from the others in the group. When he looked at one of them—Remy, he thought the great man was—he was pointing something at him and Dragon paused.

"You are trying to kill me?" He told him he was not, but he was taking his picture. "A device to capture me then. I have heard of such a thing. I should like for you to get my best side." He laughed when Remy did.

"'Tis a photograph to show Jamey and Leo what they look like with you." Dragon approved and nodded. "I think they will be pleased that you look like the two of them. And are the most beautiful dragon that I've ever seen. But it will be a while before I can let you go. I should like to ask you...you can take care of the dead, right? Make them disappear with but a flame or two?"

"I can. Shall I do that now? You will need to move back so that I do not harm you." The bodies disappeared quickly, their blood flaming brightly before becoming nothing more than a puff of smoke. Turning, he looked at the young woman that stood with her sword out and bowed before her as he touched the dead with his heat. "My lady. I did not know that you were present. Your kind has been greatly missed. I am humbled in your presence."

"You know what I am?" He nodded, shocked that she'd speak to one such as him. "Do you know a lot about me? I mean, my kind? I don't have a lot of information, as you might guess. I don't even know what I can do until I tumble into it."

"Your kind has been around my whole life. You are the reason that we exist. Your forefathers are the ones that created Dragon. To ride and soar through the sky to see where they could find more magic." She nodded. "You are a welcome sight to this old man. But as for what you can do, I am sorry, but I have as little knowledge of your magic as I do my own. It has been many decades since I've been around another dragon."

"I'm just glad that you're here. This has been a horrific war, and I think…. We were losing this, I believe." Dragon looked around, then back at Remy before bowing to him as Remy continued. "Even as long as I have been on this earth fighting them, I've not seen them lessen at all."

"It will end. Someday you shall look back upon this and wonder why you were so afeared." At least Dragon hoped so. He wanted to be free to fly again, and knew that it would not be as easy with so much work to be done. "I should like to fly, my lord. My masters would…they need a ride to air off the stench of this night."

Remy told him to go and to enjoy the night. Dragon started to turn to go to safer grounds when his lordship called him back.

"Your name? What is it?" Dragon told him that he had no such thing and that he'd been Dragon his whole life. "You need a name. Dragon is what you are. You need a name that we can call you by. You think on that and we'll call you whatever you wish."

"My masters, they will decide for me." Remy nodded and moved away with the woman that was his mate. He watched the other couple move away as well. Love was there, with both of them. He wished his own masters were to have such a thing.

Dragon moved to the open field several miles away before he spoke to the masters. "When we take to the skies, it will be frightening at first. For me as well. I have not been in flight ever before. And I will need you to tell me when you are too frightened or do not like something."

"Can we separate from your body?" Dragon told Leo that he didn't think so, but he was learning as well. "We'll have to figure this out and soon. We could do more work should we be three instead of a single, even though you did more work than we did in a month."

"We will be a great warrior either way. And I will protect you as you will me. I have a better understanding of my abilities but not a great deal. I am but a newborn dragon and have very little knowledge of me or my body." Leo laughed. "You find me humorous, sire?"

"Not really. I was thinking that for someone your size it's kind of scary to think you have no control over your movements. You know that we have no idea what we're doing either."

They played in the field for several hours. He was never able to get off the ground more than a few feet, but he could feel the happiness of the masters as they worked with him. Twice he fell to the ground, not hurting any of them but leaving a big dent in the ground beneath him. Lady Jamey said that he'd make a nice pool man should he ever want to do that. He had no idea what a pool man was or what he did, but he laughed with them. Their laughter was like music to his ears.

When he realized how tired they were, he felt badly for keeping them out for so long. But when he tried to tell them that, Lady Jamey told him that it was the most fun she'd had in ages. Leo told him he was tired but felt like it was a good ending to the day.

When they parted ways in the house a few minutes later, his body becoming his master while a part of him, larger than before, stayed with his lady, he was confused and not sure what to think about them. Did they not realize that they were united now and that sleeping apart meant a weakness to him?

My lord, do you not care for your mate? Leo didn't answer him as he stood under the spray of water. He knew that it was a shower and could see him in the glass across from him. Otherwise, Dragon would never know what happened to the human that held him. He asked him again.

"I don't want a woman in my life. Not necessarily her, but any woman. I've had my heart torn out enough, thanks." Dragon studied the muscle within his master's chest and wondered what he meant. "CarolAnn took what I would have had for Jamey, and left me with nothing but a shell of what I was."

You did not love her. Leo said that he had in a way but not like he should have. *Then I do not understand. You will close your heart to a woman that would die for you, love you above herself, and will serve only you? That does not seem like a good thing to do. Even without me in this. We need balance, as you have seen today.*

"You don't understand." Dragon told him nay, he did not. "I'm not going to let her into my heart for the simple reason that I no longer have that part of me that can love a woman. Or trust one. Jamey is aware of this and she's fine with our arrangements."

I do not think you understand her at all then. She is.... Dragon reached for the woman in question and found that she was standing near a window crying. *Nay, my lord, you do not understand your mate at all. Nor, sadly, do I think you want to.*

"What the hell does that mean?" Dragon didn't answer him, but he could feel his anger. "You have no idea what CarolAnn did to me. You need to mind your own business and keep your mouth shut about her."

As you wish. Dragon moved the part of his body that would talk to Jamey to her. He had not even realized that he could do that, but wanted to be with her and felt his shifting of his body. When he entered her mind to see what she was thinking, he was surprised at the sadness he saw there.

"I'm going to go out and set up a target for a while." He moved with her through the house, their connection stronger than before. When she encountered the faerie, she said that she'd come with her and they were in the yard in no time. He could feel the moon settle on him as the sun had today. They worked with a bale of hay set up when the faerie spoke.

"Your dragon knows what I am." Jamey asked her what that was. "I'm an earth faerie. I can control the elements. Not that I have a clue how to do it, but there you go. Hector is looking for some information so that I can figure this out. I asked the dragon, but he said that he didn't remember."

"He's very old." Dragon felt his pride in his lady master as she continued to tell stories about his life. "When I was small I thought that everyone had this being inside of them. My dad said that he was just not real and that I should never tell anyone that he was there. He didn't understand it either. But I knew that my dragon was real and the stories he told me kept me from being hurt when the other kids rejected me."

"Kids are cruel, I think." Dragon remembered the taunts that young Jamey had endured and his heart hurt for her. "What's with you and Leo? He's...I didn't think that he was going to take you for a mate."

"He hasn't. And to be honest, I don't want him either." Dragon felt his heart shudder in fear. "The man is a hard piece of work and I don't want him in my life any more than he wants me. We're not...compatible. I don't understand what this other woman did to him, but I'm thinking she had it right not to want him."

He felt her fear and started to reach for his lordship, but when she relaxed he wondered what was going on. There was a loud noise and then he felt others coming to them, including Leo. The large vehicle with a trailer attached pulled up close to the house and the being stepped out with his hand stretched forward.

"Howdy." A stranger, and he was also something that Dragon hadn't felt in the household before. "I'm Richard Harmon; everybody just calls me Rich. I guess you guys are expecting me."

"We were actually." Remy moved to stand beside the stranger. "You have yourself a load there. What do you have?"

"Drugs."

~~~

Leo had tried to take the huge box from Jamey, but she kicked him in the shin and told him to fuck off. He had no idea what to say to her about that but left her alone. They were nearly finished with the first truck of drugs and things, and they still had two more containers that had been hooked to the truck to unload yet. Then he was going to sit her down and talk to her. Jamey was taking this all wrong.

Remy was talking to Rick as they opened the next container. "This is going to help us a great deal. I can't believe that you got all this just coming along the road toward here. How did you find us anyway?"

"There was this sort of beacon in my head. Oh yeah, met up with some woman with Chris Alexander too. She is a piece of work, and he was trying to get rid of her before they got here. I had to get away from them. Never met a more vain dumb woman in my life. But she was looking for you." Rick pointed to Leo. "She said that you hurt her by not being dead, and said you owed her some money. CarolAnn Rivas is her name. You know her?"

"She's really coming here?" Rick nodded as he pulled another box from the truck and set it on the ground. "What the fuck for? To finish what she started?"

"Don't know. But she said that you owe her an insurance policy that you didn't fulfill. Sort of got the feeling that you were in deep shit about this. Oh, and she's got this lawyer telling her that she should just give up on it, that you're fine and dandy last he heard. You look fit to me."

Leo wanted to hunt her down and strangle her. But he took the next box in the house. The elevator that he was sure hadn't been there before was nearly full, and he pushed the button and watched as it made its way to the sub levels before he made his way outside again.

Rick had gone into a grocery store to stock up on water, he told them. He also said that he'd had no idea how long it would take him to get to them, but he thought that water would be something that he could bring or trade for a meal. But the rows and rows of meds had called to him.

"Bagged up as much as I could off the shelves. Then when I turned to go, there was all that shit behind the counter, the stuff the pharmacy had hidden back behind the locked wall. Had to figure out a way to keep them separate, so I put the over the counter stuff in black bags when I had them, and the prescription stuff in boxes." He laughed. "Never dreamed that I'd find so much. But it would be needed, I guessed, and the closer I got to here, the more I could see that people were dying anyway. Might have been a lost job."

"No. We have plenty of people here that could use the meds." Remy looked at Leo, then back at Rick. "You aren't human, are you?"

"Nope." Leo didn't think he was going to say anything else, but he finally did. "Vamp. You have a problem with that?"

"Not so long as you don't feed on anyone that doesn't want you to." Rick nodded, then looked at Leo. "I'm not sure what to tell you the rest of us are. I'm not human and have been around for centuries. My mate and I have only just met. Leo there has a dragon that he uses, as well as a mate."

"Dragon?" Leo nodded. "Thought so. I won't take what's not offered, but what I wouldn't give for a taste of dragon. It'll go a long way to bringing out the best in me."

"And what sort of best is that?" Before he could answer him, even if he would have, Vicki came out of the basement and smiled at them. Rick moved to her so quickly that it was seconds before Leo realized that he'd been about to bite her. But Rick's ass ending up across the yard made him realize that Davis had been close enough to protect his mate.

Neither man moved. Davis stood over Rick, and he could see that both of them, their beasts and their men, were just on the edge. It wasn't until Jamey moved to stand between them, facing the big vampire, that Davis took a step back.

"She's not to be touched." Rick nodded, and Leo made his way to Jamey. "You come near her or even look at her funny, and I will bring a hell down on you that will be second only to the end of the world. You get me?"

"I do. I had no idea that...faeries are all gone." Jamey looked at Leo, then turned her back to him before Rick laughed. "I guess that was wrong of me too. You're a dragon as well."

"For now." As she moved away from them, Leo touched his hand to her arm. The power surging through him nearly took his breath away, and he tightened his fingers on her arm to hang on. "Let me go."

He had to have her. Now. Pulling her along behind him, he entered the building. Leo was thrilled to death that she didn't fight him. Not sure what he might have done if she had, he pressed her body against the wall of his room. Trying to kiss her nearly got him unmanned.

"I want you." Jamey nodded and pulled her shirt up over her head. He moved to kiss her again, and she yanked his head back by a handful of his hair. "What the fuck is wrong with you?"

"No kissing." Leo took a step back from her. "You can fuck me all you want, but I told you, no kissing me."

"That's the stupidest thing I've ever heard." He put his hands on either side of her body and nuzzled her neck. "It's just a kiss. A meeting of lips. Bodies together. Let me taste you."

"No." Jamey rolled her hips to his, and he felt her need. When she cupped his cock in her hands, he rocked hard into her palm while making his way to her breast. Christ, he was so hard and needy that he wasn't sure he was going to make it. "Fuck me, Leo. Give us what we both need and leave me alone."

Leo lifted his head from her breast and looked at her. She was crying. When she turned from him, he pulled her face back to his and stared at her until she looked at him. He could see the pain there and hell, he could even feel it.

"What it is? What's wrong?" She told him nothing. And when she squeezed his cock with her fingers, he backed up again. "No. What's wrong with you? Is it because you think that we're mated? That I should let you into my heart?"

"You don't have a heart, Leo. Remember? That other woman, the one you compare me to, she owns it." When he took another step back, he watched her pull her clothing back around her. He started to deny that anyone held his heart but him, because it was twisting up in his chest when she spoke again. "I've done some really stupid things in my life. But none of them compare to me loving you. Yeah, I love you. Stupid me. I don't even like you, but I fucking love you."

Long after she left, he was still standing there. The dragon in him tried to talk to him several times, but Leo was ignoring him. All he could think about was that Jamey loved him. Something that he not only didn't want but had no idea how to deal with. It wasn't until Remy touched his shoulder that he realized how late it was.

"You all right?" Leo nodded, then shook his head. "Yeah, got the same answer from Jamey right before she left."

"She loves me." Remy nodded. "I didn't want her to love me, but she said that she does. Now what the hell do I do?"

"Love her back? I don't know about you, but you could do a lot worse than having a woman love you. Especially one like her. She's not going to hurt you. Never going to want you to give her all your money, and so far as I can tell, the sex is fucking fantastic and it—"

"What did you say? She left?" Remy nodded and smiled. "When? And why? She can't leave here. I never said she could."

"And she needs your permission to leave here, why?" Leo flushed and Remy laughed. "You might not think you love her, but I can see it on your face. Perhaps you could take this time while she's trying to get her shit together— not sure what that means—but use this time to get your own head on straight before...where are you going now?"

"To bring her back here. The dragon needs her." Remy asked him if he did as well. "I'm not sure what I want any more. I thought...Christ, I thought I was going to be worm food by now, and here I am fighting monsters I had no idea about, a dragon is in my body that I can bring out, and not to mention I have a woman to spend the rest of my life with...one that I fucking don't understand or really need."

"Oh, you need her all right. CarolAnn is nearly here. Seems that Chris couldn't shake her, and he called ahead to let us know that she's coming. We're still trying to figure that one out. We didn't have a phone until it rang. Anyway, he said that she's coming to see why you never died. And he thinks she might be willing to help you along with that." Leo stared at Remy, wondering not for the first time why he'd ever asked CarolAnn to marry him in the first place. "Do you love her, Leo?"

He had a feeling he wasn't talking about CarolAnn any longer. "I don't know. I don't want to. It hurts too bad to have someone love you."

"It does at that." Remy moved toward him, talking all the way. "I loved my wife. More than I ever thought I'd ever love anyone or anything ever again. Then my son was born. You should have seen him. Small as my hand yet held my love in his tiny little body as if it had been there just for him. My daughters were next. Twins. Twice blessed I was. A little girl the spitting image of her mother, and the other so much like my own dearly departed mother that she took my breath away whenever I looked at her. All so young when their lives were snuffed out. No more reason than that someone wanted to hurt me. And he did."

"Hector told me that your wife was heavy with your next baby when she was killed." Remy nodded, standing right in front of him now. "I'm sorry, Remy, but I don't think this is the same thing."

"Isn't it, Leo? You willing to let her go, let Jamey go away and never see her again? You think your life will be any different after knowing her and letting her go than it was before?" Leo didn't know and told him that. "Trust me when I tell you that you're never going to find another love like hers. Not for as long as you live...and that, my friend, is going to be for a very long time."

"I don't understand her." Remy said that he'd been around for nearly two millennia and he had no more understanding of women than Leo did. "But she's going to hurt me."

"You mean like you did her?" Leo watched as Remy walked away. But he turned just before leaving Leo's room. "Stop being a pussy and go and find your mate. And show her these if you go to her."

The thick envelope landed on the floor before him. When he bent to pick it up, he realized that they were photos. Of the dragon. Smiling, he went to the garage and settled onto a bike. He had noticed that there were four of them earlier, and now there were just three. He had a feeling that Jamey had the other one.

Chapter 9

Dolin hurt. Not just his body, but his mind as well. And if this formula was incorrect, he had no idea what either of the men would do to him. Glancing over at Ward — his head anyway — he wished that he'd been the one with his head on the pike that Benton had put in the lab, and not his friend Ward.

Not that he cared that Ward was gone. The man had suffered little compared to what he was. The necklace that he'd been required to wear both day and night was draining him. And not only that, but he thought that he was being poisoned as well. Hector was true to his word. But Dolin wished that he would be done with it.

"Well?" Dolin cringed when he heard the sharp voice behind him. Daily, one or the other, Benton or Randall, would come to the work area and ask him how his progress was going. It wasn't, so far as he could see. It wasn't as if he knew what he was doing anyway. "Are you ready for the next test dosage?"

That was another thing they were doing to him. Whenever he would come up with a formula, just basically tossing things into a container and hoping for the best, he'd have to try it. Inject it into his body or eat it. Whatever they wanted, he had to do, and Dolin was at their mercy. And it wasn't killing him quickly enough.

"I have been trying to figure out this wording. Do you understand this?" Dolin held up the paper to Randall and wasn't surprised to see the man had no more idea than he did. "I don't know what some of these things are. And if they're here, in his lab, then I can't find them."

"Did you check the locked area that I showed you yesterday?" He didn't want to go there. It was where Randal had had him take all the dead when they'd gotten here two days ago. "Go there now and see if you can find any of the shit on his list. I'm going to go down to the other place and see if I can almost kill me a meth operator to help you out."

Dolin nodded and picked up the key that had been laid out for him when he'd arrived this morning. Randall told him to be quick about it, and Dolin wanted to sob. This just wasn't right. He was in charge, not that fool of a human.

"You having a good time?" He stared at Hector and then moved by him without a word. "You should know that you're never going to figure out what he wants you to do. You're not smart enough."

"Of course I'm not smart enough in this area. I have other purposes, and being a lab person isn't what I was born to do." Hector asked him what he thought he was born to do. "Rule. And I should be ruling him, not him ordering me around as if I were nothing more than...well, than a housekeeper or other servant."

Dolin was frowning when he entered the area where the door was. The bodies were stacked in neat rows along the wall and some of them had begun to rot. The smell was enough to make him gag, and he glared at Hector when he laughed. The man would pay for his treatment of him.

"What do you think to find in here, Dolin? The antidote for the poison that you've given the other realm? I assure you that you won't. You should have saved a bit of Ward's blood for that. He is the reason that those men turned the way that they did." Dolin stopped in opening the door to look at Hector. "You didn't know that? Ward's blood was tainted. Not just that, but it was the reason for the deaths here as well. When he poisoned the water that the others drank, including you, he essentially murdered this entire realm. The fact that the two of you were never killed by it, even though you drank it, is because you're from the same gene pool. But yours to a lesser degree. That might be because you don't have the same mother, we think."

"I don't understand what you mean? What pool are we from?" Hector told him that they had the same father; Ward and Dolin were stepbrothers. "No. That's not true. We have different families."

"No. You have the same DNA, something that marks you as the same yet slightly different. It's something that I only recently figured out, thanks to the humans in the other realm. They have machines that can take a formula apart, then tell you the exact compound of it and how to make it. Amazing thing, those machines. Think what you could have done with one."

"You're going to bring me one here, this minute." Hector laughed and told him he was not. "You will, Hector. You owe me. You let them kill my Mary."

"And as I've said to you before, you killed my wife. And as much as I hated that to happen, I have my son and that alone is the reason that I do not kill you quickly. Or perhaps it is why I don't want to kill you quickly." Dolin asked him if he was forever going to bring that up. "I am. You killed the one person in his world that meant more to me than my own life. Lucky for you, Ruben is still alive, as I have said, or I would not have been playing with you but killing you much quicker than I have been."

"You're not playing fair, Hector. I never knew you to be such a mean man before. This thing with your wife, it was a necessity that you should have understood already. It was for the best. You not saving my Mary? That wasn't right of you." Hector asked him why it wasn't. "Because we loved her and she was the paste that held us together. And now because you will not help me, my friend Ward is dead as well. I have more than paid for any injustice that you think I have bestowed upon you and your head."

"You'll never be able to pay for killing my wife." Dolin turned his back on Hector. There was just no reasoning with him right now, and he had to work or have his head removed. When Hector laughed, he turned to see Benton coming down the hall toward him, and the man did not look happy.

"What is taking you so long? Randall said that he sent you here an hour ago." Dolin looked at Hector, who was still laughing, and asked him if he'd done that to get him into trouble. "Who are you speaking with?"

"Hector. He's right there." Benton looked around, then back at him. "He's just there. He's come to tell me that I'm not smart enough to figure out what you need me to do. And I think I must agree with him. I have what it takes to rule you, but not to make what you want."

Dolin looked at Hector, then at Benton. Both men had been a bad part of his life, and he was, frankly, sick of them. They were no longer any use to him and had turned it so that he worked for them and not the way it should have been. Dolin started to ask him why that was when Benton spoke again.

"If you think to play me, pretend that your mind is not all there, it will not work. You made me this way and I shall have more of the same to keep me going. And from now on you will report only to me what you find. Randall is…he is not well in the head." Dolin didn't think either of them were but said nothing. "He's mad with power and will kill you should you give him the drugs to keep him that way."

"What is it these drugs will do for you?" Benton turned to look behind him, then at him again. When he lifted his shirt, Dolin took a step back from him. "What has done that to you? I should like to have some of that power. Were you human when this occurred or your monster?"

"I am not a monster. I am Master." Dolin nodded and took a step closer to Benton to look at the wound. "I need it to keep me alive. It is the only thing that has done so thus far. The woman who did this to me will pay for it. She used magic on me that I have never seen before. I need you to make me more powerful than her. And you will, or so help me I will kill you harshly."

The wound was hot with infection. Dolin was surprised by the odor that was coming from Benton when he stepped closer. It was almost as bad as the corpse behind him. But they were dead and Benton was not. At least not yet at any rate. When he touched his finger to the gaping hole that was his belly, Benton cried out but didn't back away from him.

"What did this?" Dolin wasn't watching the man. He more than likely should have been, but he sincerely wanted to know what had caused this to one of his creations. "It looks like magic. White magic which I've never seen before.

It's almost as if the man had all the power in the world at his fingertips and used it on you."

"She did." Dolin looked up at Benton and could see the anger that was there. "A woman, a lowly woman, did this to me, and I've no way of getting back at her to kill her until you come up with the right serum to make me whole and stronger."

The anger in his voice was palpable. Dolin took a step back, and in doing so narrowly missed having his head removed. When Benton took on the form of his beast, Dolin turned and ran, but not before he felt the pull of something on his leg. Kicking back, he couldn't dislodge it but felt his leg twist painfully before he fell on his body.

He looked up at Hector as he stood before him, his arms crossed over his chest. Dolin knew a profound fear then. The monster was going to kill him, and Hector might not be able to get there in time to save him.

"You can take the portal that we use to get here. Hurry, my friend." The pain in his body had him turning to look behind him. Claws as big as his body were digging deeply into his back. Hector was still there when he turned back to him. "You must not let me die, Hector. I'm meant for greatness, and you cannot let me die like this."

"Oh, but I can. And I will." Dolin's body was being drug back. Blood smeared from under him and onto the floor beneath him. "He will need to remove your head. Do you think he knows that?"

"Hector, we're friends." The pain was making it difficult for him to breathe, much less speak. His breaths were pants now, nearly making him beg for the end. But he wouldn't. Someone would need to carry on their work, and he would do it.

"We're not friends, Dolin. I would have thought you knew that by now." Hector looked over Dolin's body and smiled. "This is going to be good. But sadly, I don't think he has it in his head to kill you just yet. He's beginning to slow in his pursuit of having your body torn to bits. I think you should be able to work without legs, can you not, Dolin?"

Dolin turned over and looked down at his body. His legs were gone from the thigh down on his left leg and from his knee down on his right. He looked at the creature that was Benton as he chewed on what was left of his leg, and felt the bile in his belly start to churn up and lodge in the back of his throat. This wasn't fair, his mind screamed. Just not fair at all.

Benton grinned at him then. His teeth were sharp and covered in blood. Dolin's mind told him it wasn't real, that it wasn't his blood that dripped from the monster's teeth. But it was, and when his mind reasoned that out, Dolin let the darkness take him under.

~~~

Jamey unloaded the water from the van at the mouth of the cave. She was just going back for more when she saw Leo. He was coming up from the road on a big bike just as she reached into the back of the van for not just another case of water, but also a few canned goods that she'd been able to snatch up.

There were only about ten people living in this area now. When she'd been here a few weeks ago, there had been two dozen. One of the men told her that they'd gone out for better living conditions and then never returned. When the bike was shut off, she looked over her shoulder at Leo as she gave the man his water and food.

Ignoring Leo, she got into the van and drove to the next place, making note of what she needed to bring to them the next time. Jamey pulled up in front of the large warehouse just as Leo did. He didn't speak to her, but when she pulled out a case of the water, he did the same. They were making their way to the building when she saw the child.

It wasn't unusual to see children out and about. Most of their parents had been killed in the first wave of malefactors and they'd been left alone. Those that could get away had even made it through the second and now the third wave of monsters, so she didn't think anything about it when the child, about seven or eight years old, hid behind the tree that was just off the property.

"You ever seen him before?" The woman that was in charge of the building looked at where Jamey had nodded, but only shook her head. "He's been out there before. I don't think he's got anywhere to go."

"We don't have a lot to share with him, but I'll start putting something out for him. And a blanket." Jamey thanked her and went to the van for two more cases of water. Leo followed her.

"You going to speak to me?" For an answer, Jamey kept her mouth shut. "Okay. How many more stops do we have to make before we can go somewhere and talk?"

"I have three more stops before I have to go and refill the van. You're going to go away and leave me alone. I think you've made it pretty clear that this is the best place for me." He told her he didn't think so. "Well, too fucking bad. I love it here."

"I'm sorry." Sure, she thought, and I can fly to the moon. "I've been a real asshole, and I want to tell you how sorry I am and to try and make it up to you. Somehow."

"I'm busy. Go peddle your bullshit somewhere else." As she took the bottled water to the next stop, she thought she'd gotten through to him when his bike didn't show up when she did at the next point. Jamey tried to tell herself that it wasn't disappointment that she was feeling, but anger. The man simply pissed her off.

But as she came back from delivering food and water to this place, he was standing near the driver's side door and waiting for her. Trying to get past him only pissed her off more when he wouldn't move.

"Remy is coming with Skylar. They're bringing meds to drop off with the water. There's nothing that will harm, but some over the counter stuff for aches and pains, as well as some first aid kits that Weston is putting together to hand out to groups." She didn't ask the million and one questions that were running through her head, but moved to the passenger side and got in. She wasn't stupid enough to turn down help when things were this bad. "If you tell me where the next point is, Davis and Vicki are going to meet us there with another van of supplies. We're going to help you pass things out to these people from now on."

She gave him the address. "I didn't take the food from the compound warehouse. I have my own stash. Tell Skylar that her things are safe."

"No one would care if you did or not. We have to work together to keep people alive." She only snorted at him. "I'm working on becoming a new man. How am I doing?"

As soon as the van stopped, she got out. There was no answer that she could give him that would sound anything but mean. She wasn't a mean person. Hurt, yes, but not mean.

As she loaded her arms with the water, Davis walked beside her to the building with several bags of groceries. It looked like enough to feed the people here for a few days anyway.

"How many are in here?" She told him there had been about five dozen people, but she'd been gone from here for a few days. "I would guess that there are less and less of them all the time. What do they do? Leave and get caught by the malefactors?"

"Some of them, but not many. Most of them go out on their own. They aren't used to living like this and are forever trying to find a better way of life. There isn't one."

He asked her why she'd say that and looked over at Leo. "I think he's fallen in love with you." Jamey looked at Davis, then back at Leo as Davis continued. "He begged me to come here and help you. Even asked me to talk to you about him. You know, talk him up."

"I'm not going back to the compound. He can live there and I'll help him out with the dragon until he gets the hang of him, but I'm not going back there." Davis nodded and handed her an envelope. "What's this?"

"You. And him. The day that you guys figured out how to become the dragon, Remy took some pictures. He had Jake pull them from his phone and print them up. You should look at them." She put them in her back pocket as the little boy from before peeked around the corner of the building. "What is it?"

"Go and get the others. Something is off." He nodded and backed away from her. Jamey knew that it was the same kid. Davis told her to be careful even as he took to the sky. The kid never took his eyes off her to watch the man fly away. She felt rather than saw Leo come up beside her.

"What is it?" She told him she had no idea, then explained what she'd seen before. "We'll do this with a great deal of caution, all right? You know these people better than anyone else, so tell me, do you know if he belongs to them?"

"The woman at the warehouse said she'd never seen him before, but she'd leave things out for him." He asked her if she meant the warehouse that was fifteen miles back. "Yes. That's what made me stop and wait. Something is…it's not right."

She knew that the malefactors had used a childlike creature to try and capture them before, so when Vicki came up to her and nodded, Jamey put out her arm. She knew that Vicki also took Leo's arm because she could see him there as well. Vicki told them to guide her to where they wanted to see. The first thing Jamey wanted to see was the boy.

The building was huge, and the boy standing next to it wasn't human. He wasn't anything she'd ever seen before either. But Leo must have because he asked Vicki to take them to the back side of the building and to look what might be there.

"Christ." Yeah, Jamey thought, Leo had that about right. "Where the fuck have they come from?"

"Don't know. But if you want me to pull back, I can or we can look beyond the building." Jamey told her to go into the building. "But I thought you were helping these people?"

"I am, but I have a feeling that something is wrong there too. How the hell did all these monsters creep up on this building and no one notice?" Vicki told her good point and took them into the building. And there they were.

"How long do you suppose this has been going on?"

The creatures were being made in something similar to an assembly line. A malefactor was shoving a piece of agate into their body and then when they didn't die, the next one was brought forth. The dead were dragged away by a group of humans, the ones she'd been helping for months, and then dumped into a large hole in the floor. There were perhaps seventy or more of the new creatures, as well as about a dozen of the workers. As they were being created, they were taken out to stand with the rest behind the building.

"They're going to attack us when we get close to them." Jamey nodded at Leo. "We could go there like the two of us and shift into the dragon to take them on."

"Wait." They both felt Vicki tense up. They had no idea what was wrong until the monster came into view. Jamey felt her own fear triple when Vicki said "It's my stepbrother."

He was a monster. And when Jamey asked her if she was sure, the thing looked right at them. His huge teeth were so sharp looking that Jamey knew that if he bit them, he'd cut them in half. As he started toward them, his big body taking flight even as he became bigger, the dragon seemed to absorb Jamey and Leo.

Her body was shifting as the dragon took them. She could feel his fear. The dragon would die to protect them, but this threat, this person, this thing in front of her was bigger, his body stronger, and his teeth sharper. When the monster took to the sky, leaving them behind to look up at him, Jamey had a sudden thought as to how they could kill it.

"Can you lift us up?" Dragon said he had no idea but he would try. "Please do. And when we're over him, let me go. I'm going to take him out with my arrows."

"No." Leo was screaming at her to let him do it, but she told him that she was the only one. "No. I can do it. Just show me what you have in mind."

By then the dragon had lifted them up. They were not as smooth as the monster was at flying, but he did manage to get them over him twice before Jamey felt she could get to him. They were taking a beating. The dragon was being torn apart, but the monster wasn't fairing much better. When she told him now, the dragon let her go.

Coming down from such a great height took her breath away. Pulling out her arrows, three of them, Jamey held them in her hand as she landed on the great creature's back. When he tried to throw her off, it was all she could do to hang onto him and her weapons. Making her way to his chest, she glanced up in time to see Leo raising his sword in the sky and bringing it down into the creature's head, just as Jamey rammed the arrows into its chest. His screams were the last thing she heard as she plummeted to the ground.

Chapter 10

Vicki sat on the ground and tried to erase the memory of what had happened from her mind. Well, not erase, but she supposed she would have to come to terms with it. Randall was dead, that much she got, but what he'd become had been what was making her mind simply refuse to see.

"You okay?" Skylar sat beside her and leaned back onto the earth. "I just left Jamey and Leo. There's no change."

"I'd never seen a dragon before that day. Not like he was at the fight." Skylar didn't say anything, so Vicki continued. "When they made him appear the other day, I think it was more of a fluke than anything, but last week when we killed all those monsters…? That was beautiful."

The couple had been there one second, but then in the next was this huge dark dragon. His great wings were on fire, as were his head and back all the way to the tip of his tail. When he lifted his arm up, his claws were hot, their heat seeming to be hotter than any fire that she'd ever been near before. And when he'd taken flight, stumbling at first until he got his feet beneath him, the dragon blotted out the sun and made them all drop to one knee in fear.

"He saved us. Not just you, but all of us. Had that monster gotten to us...I'm sorry, Vicki. I know that he was your brother, but he was going to kill us all. And had the dragon not done what he did, and then Leo and Jamey...there was no way that we could have won against something so huge." Vicki leaned back on the grass as well and thought of how to tell her what had really happened.

"It wasn't him that saved us. Yes, he did lift them to the sky, but it was Jamey that dropped from his protection. Then Leo. Had they not done that, and the dragon fought for them while they made their way to Randall's heart and head, then Randall would have killed them as well." Skylar asked her how she knew this. "When we touched...when anyone touches me and we go on our little trip, I have a part of them inside of me for a while. I knew what they were both thinking, including the dragon. He thought that they were going to die and that he'd failed them somehow. Jamey knew only that her arrow could pierce Randall's heart, and Leo's only thought was to kill him so that he'd not harm Jamey. He loves her, you know?"

"When I saw Jamey falling, I nearly went for her, to grab her up and save her, but those little monsters came out and there wasn't any time to do much more than save my ass." Vicki had fought as well and knew that what Skylar was saying was true. "They're all dead, died the moment that the monster did. Just as soon as he dropped from the sky, everything, all of them died as well."

They lay there for several minutes before Vicki spoke again. "I never told Mom. I think she knew that I lied to her before about Randall being dead, but she knows now that he's gone. I had to tell her that it was over and that she didn't have to worry about him anymore. Just…I never gave her any details, but again, I think she got it."

"The dragon in his fighting stance…have you ever seen such a thing?" Vicki told her that it was a sight she'd never forget. "Me neither. I mean, good heavens, he fought like he knew just what he was doing and that it was for us all. And gorgeous. I've never even seen one before, but I'm betting that there are none as beautiful as he is. Flames and all, he was more than I ever thought of in a dragon."

He was a combination of both Leo and Jamey. A perfect balance of the two of them. Her ability to fight with her arrows translated into the dragon having precise aim with his flame. His claws were an extension of Leo, the way that he used his sword when he was fighting. Then there was his beauty, as Skylar had mentioned.

The scales on his body were deep hues of greens and blues. The brilliance of his eyes, again, was heightened by the fact that one of them was deep blue like Leo's, the other the deepest green as Jamey's. Wings that spread as wide as a football field were incandescent even on fire, a clear blue and green that sparkled in the smallest amount of light. But it was his face that drew you to him.

"He looks like Leo, doesn't he? The dragon I mean. His face is handsome; even his shadow of a beard is his." Vicki closed her eyes and thought of the last moments of her brother's life. "The dragon saved my life."

"He did." They both lay there staring up at the sky, not saying a word for a long while. Vicki thought of the dragon, not just his looks but what he'd done, what he'd suffered to save her life.

Her brother, the monster, had been hurt. The sword in his head had not just pierced his skull but had ruined his eye as well. The milky whiteness of it had made her cry out, and that was when he looked at her. The arrow that Jamey had plunged into his heart just before she was thrown from him was covered in blood as it ran from the wound. But when Vicki had cried out for his pain, he came after her.

"You. This is all your fault." His breath was hot, his fangs, deep and covered in blood, were snapping at her as he drew closer. There had been nowhere for her to go, nowhere for her to hide. "You should have given me what I wanted and I'd not have to kill you for it."

The corner she was in was closed off. No one could have come to her, no one would have been able to save her. But the dragon, with his last breaths, had come from above, dropped Davis atop Randall, then picked her up with his claws and pulled her to safety. Davis came to her side a few moments later as she watched the dragon struggle to pull Leo and Jamey's bodies to his.

"Help him." Davis didn't want to leave her. She could see it in his face. "Help him. Maybe he needs them to live."

Davis had picked up Jamey at first. Even from where she lay, Vicki could see that she was broken. Blood covered her entire body and her arms hung limply at her sides. A long gash had lain open her chest, and Vicki was sure that she could see her rib bones, raw and broken, as well. As soon as she was laid beside the dragon, her body disappeared. Then Davis went to Leo.

He had fallen as well, but instead of being grabbed by the dragon, his body had hit the ground. When she saw him bounce once, Vicki knew that he had been killed. When Davis looked at her, she knew that she'd been right.

Taking his body to the dragon, she watched as the dragon laid his head upon the man. She saw the tears then, the big dragon mourning the loss of such a warrior as him. Vicki hurt for them all, for Jamey as well as the dragon, for the loss of her mate would hurt Jamey for the rest of her life.

"Skylar? What happens to us when this is finished? Do we go on like before, with just our regular bodies? Or do we have this...this magic I guess, for the rest of our days?" Skylar sat up, and so did Vicki. "I don't know which would be the way I'd want it."

"Me neither. But you do know that we're immortal?" Vicki asked her if that remained the same too. "I believe it does. I don't know for sure. Like most of this stuff, I'm learning like you are. But as for our magic? You will have it, I think, because you had it before all of this. Being a faerie, like you are, isn't going to change after we're done here."

"Do you think we're going to win this war?" Skylar didn't answer for a long time, and Vicki was somewhat afraid. If it took her this long to think of a way to tell her that they weren't, she really didn't want to know.

"Yes. I mean, it's going to be a while after this is done to become what we were. And I'm not sure we'd want to be that again. Not just us but everyone. There will be a lot of clean up, and sometime in the future we're going to have to think of getting things set up. I heard that Jamey had been talking to Remy about a school and some teachers. We're going to have to start over, and that is going to take some work." She stood up and gave her a hand to get Vicki up as well. "But for this war. Yes. I have to believe that we're going to win. If not, then I doubt that I'd be able to get out of bed in the morning or to go out and help kill these things. And I know deep in my heart that when this is all done, we're going to be a better place for it."

They made their way into the house, but they stopped by where the dragon had appeared a few days ago. When Leo's body had been brought to him, he had disappeared, taking them both, Jamey and Leo, with him. Now he was resting, it seemed, his big body not moving much other than to stretch out his tail or to move his head. His body was healing as well. Not quickly, but there were signs of improvement on his beaten body and wings.

"Do you think that he is healing Jamey?" No one ever talked about Leo being alive. It was a forgone conclusion that he had died when he'd fallen to the earth. "She won't stay here if she does come out of this. I don't think I would either."

"She'll stay for a time, but no, I think you're right. This place was never a home to her. She and Leo never made it one for themselves. But I think that she loved him. Very much so too."

"He loved her as well." Vicki moved away, her heart breaking for Jamey. "He wasn't nice to her. But they loved each other."

Vicki went to her room. She was still healing. Her body needed rest and Remy had told her to stay at the compound for a few more days. Davis had told her if she was a good girl that he'd make it worth her while if she was in bed when he returned. The men had gone out to get supplies for the shut-ins that Jamey had been helping. There were a great many of them, and they had started using a semi to take things.

Lying down on the bed with the thought of reading for a while, Vicki closed her eyes for only a moment before she felt her body relax enough to sleep. Smiling, she wondered what Davis would do when he found her just where he wanted her.

~~~

Remy was just coming out into the yard when a car pulled into the lot. He knew that they had to be safe or the barrier would have stopped them from coming in. When a very tatted man got out, Remy thought it was Chris but wasn't entirely sure. The man was alone.

"Chris Alexander. You're Remy." Remy said that he was and put out his hand to shake when the man did. "That woman, she's out there in another car. Safe so long as she does what she's told, but I doubt that she'd listen to anyone anyway."

"She can't get in with ill will in her heart." Chris nodded and leaned against the car and looked around. "You're here to fight with us. Hector told me a while ago to expect you."

"Hector? I don't think I know him." The man was shirtless, and before Remy could ask him why, the man smiled at him. There were fangs there and when he stood up, Remy took a step back. "I'm a cat. Panther. I...I guess you could say that I'm a cat on steroids. The fangs didn't come until recently. But I'm running hotter than I can cool off in the air conditioning in the car. I've burnt up two since I started out here."

"I see." Remy didn't, but he led the man to the compound. "Hector is the man in black. He's the one—"

Remy realized he was talking to himself when he turned. The man was staring at the dragon and then at the man standing next to him. As he made his way to the two of them, Remy had a feeling that this was going to be good. And as soon as Hector turned to Chris, he shifted to his cat, a large panther, and attacked Hector.

It took him some time to tear the two of them apart. Chris was out for blood, and Remy thought for sure he'd take any he could get. When Vicki came out and snapped her fingers, Chris dropped to his belly and whimpered.

"What did you do?" Vicki looked at him and shrugged. "Of course not. Why should this be any different? Make sure you put it on the list that you can control out of their mind with anger panthers. That should go over well."

Remy had a list of things they could do and how they did it. Some of the things on it were something that they'd all discovered they could do, and then there were things that only a couple could do. Such as he and Skylar could shift. That had been a scary discovery as well.

He'd been in the woods on the property and he'd been thinking of a large bear that he'd killed one year for his family. They had eaten from it for nearly the entire year and had had meat to share. When someone came up behind him, all he did was think of being the monster of a bear, and he was one. Skylar had laughed at him for days when it took him nearly an hour to figure out how to shift back. And she kept asking him if the bear had shit in the woods.

Can you talk to me? Chris told him that he could. *Then I should very much like it if you told me what is going on. We're a family here and we don't go around trying to kill each other. We have enough of that going on as it is.*

He changed me. Hector looked at him and told him he'd only saved his life. *I wasn't going to die. I told him that several times. I was going to live for a long time, and he touched me and everything went to fuck.*

"To fuck?" Remy looked at Skylar when she explained what Chris meant. *I see. So your life changed in a way that you're unhappy with. I'm sorry to tell you this, but he's done that to the lot of us. And I would imagine that it was for the best. It has been for me.*

I had a life. A good one. Money to burn. I even had all the women I wanted. Remy had no idea why anyone would want more than one woman at a time and asked Chris. *Because I could, damn it.*

"And within a few weeks, you would have been as dead as a nail." Skylar corrected Hector. "Oh, as dead as a doorknob. I wasn't aware that doorknobs were ever a living thing."

That, of course, sent Skylar and Vicki into peals of laughter. It made Remy smile, but he had to deal with this or every time he turned around, Hector would be cornered by the big cat. Things were just getting stranger by the second.

Perhaps if you told me what it was you were going to die from, I can better understand what we're dealing with. The big cat growled at him, and Remy shook him hard. "I've had a really bad week so far, and if you continue to act like an animal, I shall have to treat you as one. Tell me."

"Unlike the rest of you, he was in good health. And he is right in what he said about having everything that he needed or didn't need. But he was set to have a horrific accident. One that would...he would have killed several more in his haste to get to a concert that he was to be showcasing." Remy stared at the black cat when he settled down and then let him go. When he didn't move, Hector continued. "It would not have been completely his fault, mind you. The car that would have hit him would have knocked his car into a railway car's path, which would have derailed the train and killed over two hundred people. In his grief he would have taken his own life, and I had a need for him."

"Did you tell him this?" Hector said that he'd tried, several times, until it was no longer safe for him to be around the young man. "So you left him alone to deal with this on his own. I suppose that when Nathaniel gets here, I'm going to have to keep him from killing you as well?"

"Nay, Remy. You will need to keep him from killing himself." Remy started to ask him what that meant, but there was a sound behind him. Then there was a scream, a woman's scream.

The cat stood up and turned his back to them all. Remy drew his sword when a low viscous growl emanated from Chris's throat. When the rest of them drew theirs as well, Remy noticed the hair on the back of the cat's body was standing on end. Whatever was going to happen, he was going to be ready for it.

The woman that seemed to part the malefactors looked at them. He supposed that they looked a little odd. A man dressed all in black alongside a huge black panther. Remy had spread his wings in anticipation of whatever came to them and so had Skylar. Davis was there as well with his sword drawn and at the ready, as was his mate. But it was the woman that had them all standing on full alert. The woman that had none of them putting away their weapons, but remaining ready.

"Well?" She crossed the line, but it didn't make him any less fearful of her causing them harm. "Where the hell is he? I was told he was alive and here. I want to talk to him about him leaving me with nothing. That was most unfair of him to take his insurance policy and leave me. I have lost my home, my car. I can't find my sister so I can get some money from her. She should know how this is affecting me, all this being poor. I wasn't meant to be without. This has been a...are those wings on you? How much did those cost? I want—"

"Who?" Remy had a feeling he knew who she was talking about and also who she was, but there was always someone trying to get to them by lying. "We have many people here. Which person are you referring to?"

"Leonard Earl, my supposed to be dead fiancé. I've heard that he's here and living it up. I demand that you bring him to me right fucking now. I've had a really hard time getting here and I just want him to finish this and let me get on my way." Remy reached for Skylar when she started forward. "Oh, you don't want to go there, my dear. I really will make Leonard kick your ass. Provided he's not still sickly. He's not, is he? Christ, I don't want to be around him if he is. Just tell him that I want my policy taken care of now. If he wants he can give me a check for it, but have him make it out to cash. I'd rather have cash, mind you, but I'll…what are you staring at?"

"You. You're not as…put together as you once were. What policy would that be?" Rick crossed his arms over his chest as he moved in front of her. "All the way here, all you talked about was this policy and how Leo had taken it from you. How is it that it belongs to you and not his own wife?"

"Wife? I'm going to be his wife. Just get him." She had taken a step toward Rick but backed up when he seemed to grow in size. "You aren't a nice person. I don't care for people who aren't nice to me. You should know that I've called my attorney about you. He said…well, it doesn't matter what he said."

"He told you that to fuck with me is going to get you killed. And he's right. It will." Remy looked at Rick when he cleared his throat. In a low voice he grinned while he explained, "I've had a bite of her until I realized that she wasn't worth the trouble. Bitter blood and all."

He'd drank from her. Remy wasn't prudish or anything like that, but he did wonder if he'd also had sex with her. The woman looked to be like one of the kind that had followed the war to get a coin or two from the soldiers who were far from home. Most of them took back to their wives a great deal more than they had left with. Sexually transmitted diseases would kill a person during his time.

"Bitter blood?" They all turned to Hector when he asked. "I understand that she is…well, what she is and all, but what do you mean her blood is bitter?"

"She has a bite to her. Like…I guess it might be like old blood, but that's not it. Old blood or even blood of the dead will kill me." Rick looked at CarolAnn, then back at Hector. "Right? Her blood just tasted that way because she's a bitch and not because it's old?"

"Neither of those will kill you now. But if she tasted bitter, she isn't human or she's been tainted. I would say…not that I have tasted her myself, but I would imagine that she has been sent here by someone else. Changed at some point along the way." Remy asked why she could get across the barrier. "Because she has no idea what she is. She might be angry at our Leo, but she is too…I would say that she is too stupid to harm him. No matter what she says."

"Hey. That's not nice. I've gone to college." They all looked at CarolAnn. "I was there an entire month, and I did learn a great deal too."

"I'll just bet you did." Skylar just laughed when CarolAnn lunged for her. "I'd really like for you to try something. I've had a really crappy day, and taking it out on you would give me the greatest pleasure."

"I want to get back to the part where she's been tainted. We have to figure out…is that why she's been able to get by the malefactors? I would think that she'd be changed by now, don't you? And if she has been tainted, what the hell do we do to find out who sent her here?" Remy hated this, not knowing what was going on and worse yet, how to deal with it when it got here. "How was she tainted?"

"I don't know." Remy growled and everyone backed up. Hector continued before Remy could unleash his temper on the lot of them. "We can find out. We'll have to let her in the compound but watch her. And I think it might help us all if she doesn't find out that Leo is dead."

Remy was trying his best not to think of that as well. The man had saved them all with his life. He was worried about Jamey and what was going to become of her, but no one had talked that far ahead just yet. They wanted her to heal, however that was happening too.

"We'll let her in the compound, but we'll have to have some sort of barrier around her. We don't want her wandering around." Skylar said that she'd already taken care of it. "Good. Someone...she smells. I think we should find her something to wear that doesn't reek of body odor and then have her shower. I believe it might have been a while since she's had one."

"Save her clothing." Remy nodded at Chris, who was just pulling on his shirt. The man seemed to be forever without all his clothing on. "When she was with me—not like, with me with me, but when we were in the car together—she was running hot. Maybe there is something there. I think when I was with her, she radiated more heat than me."

After she was let in, Vicki and Skylar took her to the clinic. She didn't appear to be sick, but they wanted her to be checked out. Not to mention, Remy needed to get away from her. There was something about her—not just her highborn ways—but there was something about her that made him want to murder her. And that wasn't like him. Not with a person anyway. He decided that he needed more time with Skylar and went to find Ann so she could fix them a picnic lunch to enjoy alone. Maybe they all needed more time out of the building doing things they loved.

Chapter 11

Jamey opened her eyes, and when she realized how dark it was, she started to panic until someone spoke to her. It was her dragon. He told her that he had her, and that he'd never let her go again.

"You had to. Had you not...well, you had to." He didn't answer her and she reached out. Jamey had no idea what she wanted but knew for some reason that it wasn't there. "He's dead, isn't he?"

Who would that be, my lady? The monster? Then yes, he is most assuredly dead. When he died, the monsters that came with him, they too were killed. It was most...brilliant of you, I would say, but also the scariest. Should you have died, I'm not sure what I would have done with myself.

"Leo. Is he dead?" He told her he was not. "Where is he? He...I don't feel him here...where the hell am I anyway?"

You are...you are not going to like my answer, my lady, but it was the only way that I could save you both. Your wounds were terrible...should you not have been brought to me, you would have died with the monster. But Leo, his wounds were...he was dead, my lady. Dead as the monster you fought. In order to save him I had to work some magic. Some that I had no idea that I even possessed.

"Where am I?" Jamey tried to move but wasn't able to. Her body felt bound up, tightly cocooned into some.... "Dragon, where the fuck am I?"

Just where you think, my lady. You are within me. I have taken you into my body to heal you. I know not what it will do to you, but you are not dead. And that is all that really matters to me. Leo is...he is there as well, but he is deeper within me. Separate from you so that he could heal as well. Jamey felt like she couldn't breathe, and her heart started to pound. *My lady, you are doing neither of us any good, not Leo nor me, if you harm us.*

She stilled, trying to control her fear. "I'm not very good in dark places. And knowing that...tell me something. Anything. And start with when I can be released."

She felt the difference immediately. Opening her eyes, Jamey looked around the room and realized that she was in her bedroom. The one at the compound. Sitting up, she reached for Dragon and felt his laughter.

Master Leo is most upset with me. He thinks I should have brought you to him. She didn't ask him where he was but tried to think what she was to do now. She and Leo weren't the best of friends. *He wishes for me to take you to him, Lady Jamey. I would very much like to do so. It will go a long way to helping him stay still and become less restless.*

"All right." No sooner than she said it she was standing in front of Leo. He looked...well, horrible came to mind. He was laying there, his body bruised and broken. She moved to be closer to him. "Where are we?"

"I think...you know, I have no clue. But you're here now and that's all I care about." He brushed his fingers over her cheek, then over her lips. "I've been so worried about you. I woke up…I don't know when, but it seems like forever ago. And every time I could, I'd ask him where you were and how you were doing."

"I'm better. You look like you could use some more rest. Why don't you lie down?" Leo took her hand, and she went with him. There was a bed there that she was sure wasn't there before, and when he lay down, she got in beside him. Before she could ask him anything, he pulled her to his body and held her. "You were dead, Dragon told me."

"I was. I think that I knew that on some level when I jumped to help you, there was no way I was going to survive. Randall is dead. I did see that." She told him that Dragon had told her that as well. "I love you, Jamey. I don't expect you to believe me, but I do. I've been an idiot and a prick."

"No, I don't believe you. You can't love me, Leo. You hated me a great deal." He kissed her then, his mouth seemingly consuming hers. When he pressed her back against the bed, she pushed him up with her hand. "Leo, I'm here to help you rest, not have sex."

"Oh, we're going to rest. Just as soon as I make love to you until neither of us can move." He kissed her, taking her breath away once again. His hand on her breast made her breath catch. "I want to taste every inch of you. Then when I think I've had my fill, I want to start again."

Leo made his way to her breast, suckling the tip hard until she was sure she was going to come from just that. But when he bit her, Jamey screamed out her first of what she was sure was going to be many more. Leo looked down at her when he moved down her body.

"I've been thinking of you naked and under me for days now. I'm going to eat your pussy like it's a feast. Then

I'm going to make love to you with my fingers over and over until I'm no longer thirsty for you. By then you will be ready for me." She told him she was ready now. "Ah, but not for what I have in mind. I'm going to flip you over, fuck you from behind while I drink from you."

"Leo, this isn't resting." His grin told her that he didn't care. She was pretty sure that she didn't either. And when he sat on his knees between her legs, she sat up enough to look at his body.

"You were hurt so badly." He wrapped his hand around his thick cock, and her mouth watered. "Do you think this is a good idea? I don't want you to be hurt more."

"This is the best idea I've ever had. Spread your legs for me, Jamey. Let me look at how wet you are for me." She did as he asked, shy about what he was seeing yet extremely turned on by the look on his face. "Christ, am I going to enjoy this. I might not ever stop."

Leo moved down her body, touching her everywhere with his free hand, keeping his cock slick with his hand with the other. Jamey wanted to taste him, take him into her mouth and have him release there. But when he ran his fingers over her wet curls, it was all she could do not to beg him to take her now.

His mouth seemed to be everywhere as he lay down. She knew that he was biting her, she could feel the bite of his teeth every time he did it. But she also knew that he'd never hurt her. Not for any reason. When he slid his finger into her, his thumb pressing against her swollen clit, Jamey begged him to finish her now.

"Not yet. I'm not ready for you to come just yet. I want to play a little first." His tongue swirled around her clit as his thumb touched her so indecently. "You're so wet. And smell so delicious."

Jamey came as soon as he sucked her clit into his mouth. Curling her hand into his hair, Jamey was going to pull him away, give herself a much needed breath, but he slid his fingers into her again and again until she was screaming out a second then a third powerful climax. If he kept this up, she'd be dead before he was inside of her. And Christ, what a way to go, she thought.

Over and over, he brought her to such heights to let her barely fall all the way before he was bringing her up again. Her body bowed up in response to his tongue inside of her. She came when he told her to squeeze her breasts, pinch her nipples. When he lifted his head, she was sure he was going to take her, but he sat back on his knees and fisted his cock quickly.

"I'm going to come like this, see my cum all over your body before I take you." Sitting up, she wrapped her hands around him. He was thicker than she remembered; his cock was hot as well. "If you keep that up, I'm going to come sooner than I wanted."

Jamey took him into her mouth. She didn't ask him if she could, didn't even care if he wanted her to or not. But she knew that if she didn't taste him, and now, she would not be able to go on. His hand at the back of her head gave her all the encouragement that she needed.

Leo tasted of hot spice. Honey too. Licking a long path from his tip to his groin, she moaned when he did. Cupping his balls in her hand, Jamey felt their weight and wanted to feel their hot juices slide down the back of her throat. Sucking just on his crown, then taking as much of him into her mouth then down her throat as she could, Jamey swallowed. His cry out that he was coming was all the warning that she got before he started to pound the back of her throat.

Leo held her to him as he emptied into her. Before she could be satisfied that she'd given him release, he had her on her belly and her ass up to his cock. When he slammed not into her pussy as she had expected but into her ass, Jamey came again, her entire being seeming to be coming apart only to be put back together to do it again before he bit her on the shoulder.

"Come."

Jamey screamed when he commanded her to release. She had no strength left, she'd thought, no way to be able to release so many times, but she did. Her body came again as she slid her own fingers into her pussy, his there as well, tugging and pulling on her clit to bring her again. And when Leo came, his cum filling her ass as he had her throat, she came just as darkness seemed to be just on the edge of her vision. When things blurred then snapped into focus again, she knew that she would love him forever.

Jamey fell to the bed, her body no longer able to hold her up. Leo fell atop her and she heard him laugh. Turning so that she could look at him, he kissed her nose and rolled to his back. She rolled over and looked down at him.

"I had no idea that we would enjoy that so much. I've never...did I hurt you?" She shook her head no and asked him what had been so funny. "Us. We seem to...I don't know. Go for the very violent in all things. Are you sure I didn't hurt you?"

"You didn't. I enjoyed that as much as you did." Laying her head down on his chest, she wondered where they were going to go now. "You have to rest, Leo. I don't know where we are, but I'm pretty sure that the others are worried about us."

"You, they're worried about you. And I've heard them. Remy has been with the dragon a few times. He thinks, like everyone does, that I'm dead." Jamey sat up and looked at him. "I was dead. I know that. And someone, I'm assuming the dragon, brought me here. He said that I'm within him and that something might change with me when I'm released."

"Released how?" Leo shrugged and she lay back down. "I don't think I want any more changes to me."

Leo ran his hand up and down her back. It was both relaxing as well as very sexy. When he lingered along her ass, she moved her body up so that he could touch her if he wanted, and his fingers slid into the seam of her bottom then back up again.

"I want you again." Moving over him, Jamey sat on his cock. Using her fingers, she played with them both, her pussy and his cock, until he told her that he needed to be inside of her. Sitting up on her knees, she slowly lowered herself onto his hard cock. "Ride me, Jamey. Come by riding me."

"You're so thick. Bigger than you were before." His fingers dug deeply into her thighs when she started to move her hips. "I could come like this, riding you while you're holding me."

When he sat up and took her breast into his mouth, she held him to her. Christ, he was giving her such pleasure that she was sure she'd die from it. When he cupped her ass, bringing her body to his while she moved, her clit touched him in ways that had her riding him quicker.

"You like this." Nodding, she moaned when he slid his finger into her ass. "Do you have any idea what I felt when I came into your tight ass? It was paradise. Like nothing I'd ever felt before."

"Leo, I'm going to come. Christ, yes. I'm coming." She did too, screaming out his name over and over. When he pulled her mouth to his throat, tilting it in a way that made her realize what he was wanting from her, Jamey felt her fangs stretch in need to sink into him. When she did, she came hard again, screaming around his flesh.

His blood was delicious—like his cum, spicy and hot, but this was making her feel like she could soar. Her body felt stronger for it, and when he took her wrist to his own mouth, she felt him bite her deeply, bringing her once again over a summit that she knew she'd never be able to forget for the rest of her life. This time when she felt the darkness take her, she let it, sliding into it like the welcome arms of a lover, like Leo.

~~~

Leo watched her sleep. He couldn't let her go, not for any reason. And he wouldn't. Not ever again. When someone touched his mind, he knew it was Dragon and welcomed the intrusion from his good friend.

She is well now. As are you. Tomorrow you may return to the living world. Leo started to ask him where he was now but the dragon spoke again. *Do not ask me, for this is all new to me. I've not an idea where you are. I only know that I asked of the earth to help me save you, and she responded that she would do all that she could. She told me that you would be a part of me. Beyond that, my lord, I have no idea.*

"I love Jamey, Dragon." Dragon told him that was right. "I never wanted to love anyone. Not...I never loved CarolAnn. Especially not like I do Jamey. She's my everything." He laughed at how good it felt to not just say that, but to mean it as well.

And you are hers. There will never be another like her. Or you. My dragon will be the only one as well. We will live on forever. Leo stroked Jamey's cheek before getting up. He was suddenly very hungry. *You will improve much now. Her*

154

blood will give you strength that you could not have gotten from our magic.

There was a refrigerator in the room now, as well as a table and two chairs. Wherever he was, wherever they were, it was much like the compound in that it would accommodate him with whatever he needed. Taking out a large platter of chicken, Leo sat it on the table and thought of a glass of wine. When it, too, appeared on the table, he smiled. This was something that he could get used to, and thanked the dragon.

It is not I, my lord, but you. You and your mate have more power than I do. A different magic than I. More than…more than I have ever seen in a couple. Leo asked him how that was possible. *I don't know the answer to that. You just are. The others, Remy and Skylar and the rest of the men and women at the compound, they are stronger as well. But I do not think they know it as yet. And I am as well. I never thought to separate from the two of you. We are one, or so I thought.*

"You mean that you can be free of us? Work alongside of us and not just with us?" Dragon told him that he thought so. "How is that…? Never mind. I'm sure you don't know that any more than I do."

I have not spoken to Remy on your wellbeing. He isn't aware that you live. I shall tell him now so that he might be prepared. I do not believe that the two of you can talk, but then I wasn't sure that you and I could either. But we are…evolving, I think. I do have some news for him, but I will wait until tomorrow. There is trouble brewing on this earth that he will need to be made aware of soon. Leo asked him what it was. *The monster has another. A man that was once just as Remy is, he is evolving as well. But his mind has not. A warrior without a family, but different too. Remy is a man that is much loved and respected. This man is not.*

"Benton?" Dragon told him he only knew him as Master. "Do you know where he is? To be honest, I thought he was dead."

Nay, not dead, but his mind is corrupted as I have said. He has been taking many things into his system that has made him quite mad with anger. He is most...how shall I say...? He is most angry with Remy and Hector. His anger is well beyond what a mind such as his can deal with. It will not come to a good end for him should he try some of the things that he is thinking.

"You have a connection with him?" Dragon told him it was a connection that he'd gotten when he and Jamey had killed the other monster. "You mean because we killed him, then you can see and hear what he's thinking?"

"I know his every thought, though I must confess, some of them are very confusing. And not just when you killed him, but his blood touched yours. The lady of the earth said that the soil there, where he fell, would be dead for more years than she's been living. I do believe that to be a very long time."

"I bet." Leo got up to pace, his snack left untouched as he tried to wrap his mind around what dragon was saying. "You need a name. You're going to have to think of one, please? One that you like."

Remy told me the same thing a few weeks ago. Said that dragon is what I am, but it does not have to be what I'm called. I have given it some thought. I have narrowed it down. When I have a choice, I will tell you. Leo thanked him. *Sire, you should see what you can see of this man's mind. If I can see it, perhaps you and the lady may as well.*

Leo wasn't sure he wanted to do that. Not because he didn't want to see the other man's mind, but he really wasn't prepared to have much more magic bestowed upon him just now. He continued to pace until he smelled, rather than heard, Jamey come into the room. She looked frightened and when he went to her, he knew that they'd be going back sooner than they'd thought.

"She's there." He started to ask her who when she continued. "CarolAnn. I just talked to Vicki and she was talking about this woman that was there and how whiny and demanding she was. It was by accident, I swear. I never knew that I could do that, and now that I can, I don't know how to turn it off."

"Turn what off, love?" She was stiff with her fear, and he felt his own start to rise. Holding her in his arms, he heard Dragon say that he would return for them shortly and waited for Jamey to talk.

"I can see her. Not just see her, but right in the room where she is. You can't have wanted to marry that...never mind. That's none of my business. But ewww. Gross woman." Leo laughed and asked her if she was jealous. "Jealous? Of her? Hardly. But she's all...bubbly and stuff."

"Bubbly? I don't know about that. She was too thin if you would have asked me. And fussed too much—" He watched as Jamey stared at him, confused. "What is it you see that I didn't before?"

"She's bubbly. I don't know...let me think." He let her go when she pulled back. Her pacing was much harder than his, her feet pounding on the floor as her arms swung around and her mouth moved to a silent conversation she was apparently having with herself. "She's not human. And I know that I'm not either now, but she's so not looking human. Her hair is sticking up all over the place like she's carrying around a wind machine that is keeping it moving. But it's not quite hair, but...snakes. Is that possible?"

He had no idea. "What else did you see? Maybe this isn't her but some alien that has come to help us out."

"No, it's her. They have her confined. Like in some sort of power circle. Skylar made it." Jamey paused in her pacing and closed her eyes. He knew that she was looking at her again. "Her hair is snakes. Her face isn't really bubbly but moving, like she has something just under her skin that is making it appear to be in constant motion. Her tongue is long, not forked but sort of blunt at the tip, like there's a horn there. I don't know. Her left...no her right arm is hanging badly, like it's been broken and didn't mend right. Her left is sort of long, too long for her body, but it's scaly, like the dragon's scales."

Leo sat down. This wasn't CarolAnn, at least not the one that he'd known. Reaching out to Remy, he told him what he knew, not the least bit surprised when he asked him where the fuck he was.

I don't know. And if you ask the dragon, he won't know either. We're here to heal. That's all I know for sure. Remy told him he was glad for that then. *Me too. But CarolAnn? You have her confined I've heard. Is it safe? I mean, she's not...how did she get into the compound?*

We're working that out too. This is so fucked up, as Skylar would say. I don't think I can take much more of this unknown stuff. Did you know that we now have a panther and a vampire living here with us? And we're expecting Nathaniel any time now. I'm almost afraid to find out what troubles he's going to bring with him. Leo laughed. He couldn't help it. There were so many things going on outside of the compound, and there was enough drama to fill pages and pages of work for a sitcom within the walls of it too. He realized that he should have been paying more attention when Remy said his name like he'd said it before. *Leo, where the hell are you now? When are you coming back? Today would be just wonderful.*

I'm going to see if we can get the dragon to bring us now. I'm assuming that he has to work that out as well. Remy was cursing and Leo had to bite his lip so as not to laugh again. He thought perhaps it might get him hurt. *I think maybe you should be prepared for a few changes in us as well. Not just the dragon, but Jamey and I as well.*

There was silence on Remy's end. Leo knew that he was still there, he could feel him. So when he spoke, it was his words that startled him, not that he was speaking.

I was a simple man. I had a wife, children, and a farm. I raised prized horses and sold them for feed and grain. Once, when things were going well, I was able to buy my wife a lovely locket. I have it still, but she wore it until…until I took it from her charred cold body. Leo didn't know what to say so said nothing. *Then when they were killed, I went to a battlefield, one that I knew was a lost cause, a fight that would spill more blood than I'd ever seen up until then. I willingly gave my life to it, having the need to die to lie near my wife.*

Remy, I'm so sorry for your loss. Remy said nothing. Leo realized something in that moment…he could see his friend. See him sitting in a field with the sun beating down on his face. *Remy? Are you going to be all right?*

I do not know. I simply do not know. I would like for my days to be spent with the mate that I have now. A time of leisure, making love near a moving stream while she screams out my name. I wish for a time that I can live in a home of my choosing, where the walls do not move when I think I need more room. A place where the kitchen does not give me what I crave, a time where there are no malefactors trying to kill me at every turn. Leo felt his heart hurt for the man. He'd seen so much, suffered more than anyone. *Do you think there will be a time, Leo? A time when things are known to us? A place where we are considered normal and not monsters by the people who wish us dead?*

I hope so, Remy. I really do. Because while I've not lost like you have, I have found that I have more to live for than I ever did, and I would like to spend time getting to know her. Loving her as you do Skylar, and maybe one day having children in a safe and malefactor free world.

Come home, Leo. I have much need for you and a hug. I am not a man who gives into such things often, but I have a powerful need to have one from you. Leo told him he'd be there soon and that he could use a hug as well. *We are not a normal bunch. It is doubtful that we ever will be. Do you think?*

I think we're as normal as it gets. Remy laughed. *Jamey and I will be there soon. Dragon said that he has to work it out. As soon as he does, then I'm going to be there.*

Leo went to the bedroom to tell Jamey what he and Remy had talked about. He also told her that he was worried for his friend. Their alone time together was at an end. But they were never going to be apart again, not if he had any say in it.

Chapter 12

CarolAnn felt weird. Not sick, just weird. When the man who had been introduced to her as Dr. Weston Page came into the room again, she sat up straighter and tried to straighten her hair. Her arms, especially her left, felt like it had been sprained badly, but he told her it was fine. And no matter how many times she complained about it, the good doctor told her it was probably just a bruise. And no one, no matter what she asked, would tell her a damned thing.

"I'm wondering when I can be let go. I have to find Leonard, and he's not coming to me." That was another thing that was aggravating her. No one would look at her, not in the face at any rate. She wasn't a vain woman...well, not much...but she did like it when people, especially male doctors, noticed her. "I was also thinking that when I get this thing settled with Leonard, you and I could maybe hook up."

She wasn't sure, but she thought he said not on her life. But that couldn't be right. She was young, beautiful, and would soon be as rich as she could be just as soon as

Leonard did what he was to have done months ago. The doctor asked her to lie back down, and CarolAnn hastened to do what he asked. She would have stood on her head if he would come over here and touch her other than clinically.

"You have a very high temperature, and your blood pressure is very high as well. Have you had any flus that you can remember? Any kind of illness that would make you run a temp?" She told him no but found herself leaning into his hand. "Miss Rivas, I don't know what you think might happen between us, but you're wrong. I'm not interested in you in that way."

"Oh." She lay there for several minutes while he wrote in his chart. Then it hit her. "You're gay. Why didn't you just tell me that in the beginning and I'd have not wasted my time with you? You people need to have a mark or something."

"You mean like a number tattooed into our arms?" Nodding, she thought she saw him cringe from her. "You can't be serious. How can you think like that in this day and age? And for the record, I'm not gay. I'm a very heterosexual man. I just don't care for you."

"Not care for me?" Something inside of her seemed to move. It was like there was something in her that was much bigger than she was. And it wanted out. "I don't feel well."

"You aren't well if you think that having…what's wrong?" She tried to tell him that she had no idea when the movement in her body shifted again. When she tried to stand up, things got worse and CarolAnn reached for the bed but missed. "Just don't move. Or touch anyone."

"Well, that's just rude." CarolAnn lay on the floor. The coolness of the tile felt good on her face, and she looked at the doctor when she heard him say her name. "I feel like I'm going to puke out this other me. Not a nice one either."

"You're not nice anyway. But what do you mean, this other you? What do you think is going to happen?" This man was making her upset, but the more she got angry with him, the more the shifting in her body hurt. "I'm going to have someone take you outside. I think that's where you need to be."

"It's not nice to toss people out on their bottoms. When I'm rich, and that should be soon, I'm going to buy you out, then tell everyone what a nasty doctor you are." He didn't say anything, but she could feel herself being lifted up. CarolAnn wasn't sure but she thought she saw Leonard holding her. "Where have you been? I've been everywhere looking for you. You lied to me. You're not ill at all. And where is my insurance money? I have plans for that."

"I've told you before, I don't have any insurance policy. And in the event you didn't notice, you can't collect on it if I'm still alive." She told him she would take care of that for him as well. But something inside of her moved again, and CarolAnn had a feeling he had felt it as well. "What have you been doing with yourself? You're...who are you? But you should know this, you can't kill me, CarolAnn. Not now, not ever. And I'll live long after you're nothing but dust in a hole."

"Is everyone going to be mean to me today?" He said something, but she was suddenly cooler. "Oh, that's so nice. Yes, air conditioning. That other man would never make it cold enough for me."

"What other man?"

CarolAnn wanted him to be jealous, but she didn't hear that in his voice. Not that she was going to take him back now, but there was the issue with her money. She wanted it more than she needed him to be jealous right now.

"Where is the money? The money from when you told me you were going to die. That's mine and I want it. And you've been mean to me, Leonard. Why? What did I ever do to you?"

"I'm not going to tell you again that there is no fucking money. And you left me when I needed you, maybe? You became more interested in how it would look for you to care for a dying man than my feelings?" He snorted at her as he set her down outside. "Any of those reasons alone should be enough to have me dislike you. But really, I just feel sorry for you. And I don't really care about all the other shit now. I have someone that I truly love in my life, and realized that you really aren't worth it."

"Not worth it indeed. I'm very special. I have people who love me. And I'm beautiful." Her belly turned again. "What did those men do to me?"

She was talking out loud, she realized when he asked her what men. Trying to keep her mouth closed was difficult for her when she just wanted to scream and yell at Leonard that he was being rude. At some point she thought maybe she saw something out of the corner of her eye, but didn't look again. Moving her head was making her sick too.

"I need to get this thing out of me." Leonard backed from her, and she saw the woman then. She was with her fiancé and she didn't care for it. "Tell that bitch to get off you before I let this thing go."

"What is it?" CarolAnn told whoever had asked the question that she didn't know. "Can you remember how it got inside of you? Where you were when it happened?"

"There were these men. But one of them...he was huge." She smiled at the memory of the man. "He could fuck like he could go for hours. I think we did. But he kept telling me that when I came with him I'd be his. I came so many times that I didn't care if he came or not, but he had a huge dick."

Someone was talking, but she had no idea who it was. That person said that it wasn't him and CarolAnn looked at Rick, one of the men she'd ridden with. It wasn't him and she said as much.

"He was huge dicked. I never saw Rick's. Not that I didn't try, but this guy was hung. I think he had a dick like a foot long and at least five inches around. He was hung. Like a bull. I never dreamed he'd fit in me, but he said he would and damned if he didn't." She giggled when she remembered that he was a bull, or had turned into one. "And he had another guy with him. They both fucked me for a time. My ass was burning, but my pussy was humming."

CarolAnn giggled again. Someone was asking her questions, but she didn't know what they were saying. All she could think about was the shifting in her body and that she was beginning to hurt in places that shouldn't be hurting.

"He told me that I had to come to you. That once I was here that he'd give me a huge...huge something. I don't remember what it was." Her mind was fuzzy and she tried to make it focus. "Maybe he wants to fuck me again. I'd like that. His dick was huge."

"You said that. What did he look like other than his appendage?" That word set her off in giggles again. She had no idea who was speaking to her, but he seemed so prim and proper. "CarolAnn, what did he look like?"

"Dark hair and dark eyes. He kept calling himself Master. I had to call him that too. But I didn't care, so long as his dick was master of my pussy. But the other guy, he had the big cock. Just dripping with juices that he said would be mine. And I took it. Everywhere. His cum just about flooded me with heat and...sometimes it was so hot, I thought I was blistered. But I loved the way he fucked me. Both of them fucked me right good." On some level, she knew that she didn't usually talk like this. But she had no filter it seemed. CarolAnn looked at the man in front of her. "Leonard? Why aren't you dead?"

"I got better." That didn't sound right. He'd been close to dying. It was the reason she'd left him. "This person, Master, did he tell you what he was going to do to you? Other than the obvious?"

"Fuck me, you mean?" He nodded, and she noticed that his body looked different. "You changed yourself, so I might not be able to—"

The pain took her breath away. It was as if someone had poured hot oil over her skin and in her veins. When someone started screaming, it took her several seconds to realize it was her. And it wasn't enough, just screaming to show the pain. It was simply too much, and she felt like her pussy was being ripped apart.

"CarolAnn? What did he tell you?"

She couldn't answer. Even if she knew the answer, she just couldn't get anything out of her mouth but the pain. Looking at Leonard, seeing him she was sure for the very first time, CarolAnn had the overwhelming urge to kill him. To tear his throat out and to stomp him into the ground. But that wasn't her. She would say she would kill him, but would never harm anyone. Her body was...it wasn't hers, she realized, and grabbed Leonard by the shirt front.

"Run." Leonard backed up. "Run now."

He took another step back from her, but she was terrified that it wasn't enough. He was still much too close. Trying to crawl away from him, get a lot of distance between them, she cried out with each movement of her body. She saw the line of magic and knew that she had to cross it. Now. As soon as her body was over it, CarolAnn lay down.

Her death was coming, and quickly now. And she was more than ready for it to come and take the pain away. But every time she tried to move away from the crowd of people around her, someone would come closer to her. Then she saw her.

CarolAnn had no idea how she knew who she was, but there the woman was. And her hatred of her, the feeling of needing to lash out at her, made CarolAnn grab her arm and hold on. Looking into her eyes, she could see things there that not just frightened her, but made her feel like whatever pain she was having now would be nothing compared to what the woman would do to CarolAnn should she hurt the man she loved. And it was Leonard.

"Save him." The woman nodded. "Love him too. I can't. I can't love anyone by myself. I never could."

"I need to touch your skin."

CarolAnn wanted to tell her no, that it would be dangerous, but knew that if she did, then some of the pain would go away. And if not, then she'd kill her. At CarolAnn's nod, the woman touched her skin and CarolAnn screamed. It was the sound of breaking bones, her lungs exploding, that CarolAnn heard as she simply left her body.

~~~

Jamey touched her fingers to the woman's hand. It was almost too hot, the skin there so blistered that as she touched her, as gently as she could, they popped. Pus poured from the wound, dark in color and putrid to smell. As CarolAnn shifted and her body began to take on some other shape, Jamey moved back but not nearly fast enough.

It took the woman over, seemingly ate her. What it was, whatever had consumed CarolAnn's body, seemed to just grow and grow. The skin became not just blistered now but peeled away in great pieces. Its eyes darkened and elongated. As it held onto Jamey's arm, she had a feeling that it wanted not just her but all of them dead. Then it pulled her close enough to its head, a monstrous one that looked lizard like, and smiled.

"You should have run when she told you." Jamey felt rather than could see the others start to fight the thing. "You will be the first to die. And when you do, know that all of them, even the ones that came here to be safe, will die as well."

"I've killed one of your kind once; it won't be hard to do so again." She saw him pause, his hand around her body loosened, and she pushed hard enough to get away. But she'd forgotten about his height and fell to the ground hard, knocking her head. He reached for her again just as something huge knocked her back.

She watched as Dragon tore into the creature and fought it. She was sure that he was going to die, that he'd not be able to survive the monster that had been CarolAnn, but he didn't seem to pause. Dragon never once seemed to care about his own well-being. When she stood up, Leo pulled her into his arms. She felt it as soon as they touched. Their dragon needed them.

To say that she was surprised when they seemed to become one with him would have been grossly understated. The dragon thanked them even as he took to the sky. She thought for sure that he was leaving the others, but he turned just as he got to a dizzying height and came down, his body slamming into the monster hard, knocking him back from the barrier that kept them all safe.

The monster screamed at them as he stood up. His ability to cross the line was taken away the moment that CarolAnn had crossed it, and he'd just seemed to realize that his magic or whatever it was could no longer enable him to get to them. As they all stood there, safely within the magic of the compound, Dragon dropped to the ground. Jamey felt tossed away from him even as his large head slammed into the ground, causing the ground to shake.

Leo grabbed her up as he ran by her. The dragon was dying. Jamey had no idea how she knew this, but she did. Leo must have felt the same thing because as soon as they were within a few feet of their friend, he dropped to his knees and put his head to his.

"What were you thinking?" Tears streamed from her eyes as she saw the damage that had been done to him. Leo put his hand over one such wound as he continued. "You should have waited for us to join you. We could have helped you."

"Nay, my lord, you could not. Had you come to me sooner, we would not have been able to cause the damage that we did, or been able to push him away from the magic that will keep you safe. You must be safe." Dragon's voice was low, filled with pain that she could see. Crying, she crawled to his head, climbing over his neck to wrap her arms around him. "I will give you something that I had hoped to bestow upon you when you were stronger. But you must take it willingly. Both of you."

Jamey started to tell him she would rather have him than whatever he had, but Leo was shaking his head. "You will give us nothing that will drain you. I will not accept it from you. Please don't die, Dragon. I need you."

"You need me no longer, my lord. You are stronger now than you've ever been." He moved and looked over Jamey's shoulder to Remy. "My lord, you will need this as well. I need...there isn't much time left for me. Should you refuse this magic that I must impart to you, then it shall be wasted. Please do not allow that to happen."

"What will it do?" Jamey looked at Remy when he asked. She wanted to tell him to go away, to leave them alone, but dragon laughed and she knew that he'd picked up on her thoughts. "If it is knowledge of what we are and what we are doing, then I will gladly take it. But magic? I do not think this body can handle much more."

"You will need it. The monster now, even as we speak, is growing stronger. His magic is not his own, but he will use it in ways that will make the previous attempts to kill you seem...I am sure you will thank me later."

Jamey looked at Leo and Remy. "You will kill him." Remy told her that he was nearly gone now. "I don't want it. I refuse to take something from him that might quicken his death. Maybe we can do something else."

"There is nothing for you to do, my true heart. You have protected me for your whole life. It is now time for me to protect you." She sobbed and laid her head on his neck again. "You will go on and triumph over this monster. You must for all mankind."

"I need you." He told her that she no longer needed him because she had Leo. "Please don't leave me. What will I do, Dragon? How will I go on without you near to me?"

"You will always have a part of me within you. And should you need me, my magic and my strength, it is there for you. And will be as long as think of me as your friend." Jamey held him to her, feeling his body weakening even as he continued. "I need for you to take this, my lady. For if you do not, then all will surely be lost. And I...and I have a name. I should like to be called Bob. I so like the way it rolls from my mouth."

Jamey wanted to refuse him the magic, but the name he had chosen made her laugh. She wanted to tell him to fuck all of mankind, but knew that he was right. Maybe not the magic coming to her and what it would do, but that things would be gone and never returned if she let his magic slip through her fingers.

"All right, I'll take it, Bob."

The moment the words were out of her mouth, she felt it. Not just the strength that came to her, but the magic as well. Closing her eyes against the movement and shaking of the earth around them, she held onto Dragon. Held him tightly for as long as she could.

Jamey heard Remy cry out, even Leo's cursing, but she never let go of Bob. Holding onto him gave her peace in her otherwise upset world. And when she was fading out, her mind simply shutting down, Jamey mourned the loss of her dearest friend.

"Are you okay?" Jamey opened her eyes and looked up at Vicki. She was grinning. "Leo is over there putting together a string of words that I doubt very much have ever been put together before. I'm pretty sure that he's made up a couple of them all by himself."

"Why?" Vicki shrugged but put out her hand. Jamey was almost afraid to take it. Things had been transferred to one another on much less. "Is it safe to touch you? Or should I ask you what sort of things were done to me that you can see?"

"Nothing that I can see. You look about the same. Covered in blood and something I don't even want to think about what it might be." Jamey turned then and shook her head. "If you don't stand up soon, Leo will beat you to it, and I hate to be a loser in any sort of game."

Standing up, the touch of the woman doing nothing more than lifting her up from the ground, Jamey looked over at Leo. He and Remy were still lying on the ground and neither of them looked in any hurry to stand up. Walking to them, slowly since she was a little wobbly, Jamey looked down at the two of them.

"That dragon of yours is gone." Jamey tore her eyes from Leo to look at Remy when he spoke again. "And should he not be gone, I would go to him right now and run him through. Not hurt me indeed. Did you know that he's given me more that I don't know how to use? And not only that, I think he might have marked me a bit more. And what sort of name is Bob? Why not Robert? Bob is a...well, it is his name and we will honor him with it. But I do not like it."

"I feel like he's run me over." Jamey looked at Leo and grinned at him. "You stand there like nothing happened, when I know for a fact that you were tossed about as much as we were. Why is that?"

Jamey shrugged. "I guess I'm by far superior to you both." That got him sitting up. "Or it could be just what Vicki said. Women are better equipped to handle pain than a mere man."

Vicki, of course, had said no such thing, but she acted as if she had. "Yeah, I was just telling Jamey there that you two have been whining for over an hour about how you have a little boo-boo. Suck it up, buttercups, there is work to be done."

Skylar, not to be outdone, joined them. "You two act like little kids. Get up off the ground and act like you have a pair. Christ, we don't even have balls, but I think we have more than you do. Get the fuck up."

Remy pulled Skylar down on top of him and growled. It was funny really, to see such a huge man reduced to tickling his mate like a kid. And when Leo grabbed her, she fell on top of him and felt the hum of their magic. It felt like she'd put her body against a large high-powered battery, and she wondered if Leo was feeling the same. When he pulled her ear to his mouth and bit her, she knew that he was as well.

"I want you." Nodding, she moved her face to his neck. "Christ, if you bite me right now, I'm going to roll you to your back and fuck you right here in front of all these people."

"I want to suck your cock." He moaned, and Jamey felt lighter. "Leo, what the hell is…? Christ."

They were airborne. Not just up in the air as they had been with the dragon, but soaring up as they'd been on the ground, entwined with each other, and their wings, something they'd never had before, were lazily taking them higher.

"How are we doing this?" Jamey told him she had no idea but she liked it. But instead of staying together, Jamey separated her body from his and thought of flying alone. Her wings spread wider and she felt wonderful. Leo was doing the same and she stared at him as he moved through the sky.

"We can fly." Jamey giggled at her statement. "I guess we should have figured that we'd get wings. Vicki told me she got hers after she and Davis were together too. But this feels…. I've never felt like this before."

"Me neither." As she moved over wind currents, over trees and sailed along the ground, mostly bumping into things and breaking limbs off everything she came near, she began to get used to the way her wings worked and how her body could move with them. Landing on her feet some miles away from the compound, Leo landed beside her.

Their wings curled up but didn't disappear. As she moved forward, Jamey noticed that they moved along the ground and wondered if that would harm them. But she did think it was strange that she could feel them, her feathers, as if each one of them were a different part of her, like each finger on her hand. She said as much to Leo.

"I can feel it as well. It's like if one of them were to be plucked out of body, then it would be as painful as a nail being removed from my hand." That was something that she didn't care to experience and moved ahead of him to see the building that they'd landed near.

"What is this?" Leo told her he didn't know. "It's empty. And I don't mean of just people, but of everything. Like nothing at all inside."

When they entered, she found that she was right. There was nothing…no boxes, no furniture, not even dust seemed to cover the floor of the place. She moved to the stairs just as Leo went to one of the doors on the level they were on. Nothing was there either. As they climbed the stairs, Jamey had the strangest feeling that this place was safe. Not just safe from the malefactors, but from everything.

"I feel like this place is an extension of the compound." Jamey told him she felt it as well. "Maybe Remy or Skylar set something up here and never got around to using it." But that didn't seem right either.

Not that they were cramped for room at the compound, but every inch of it was being used. If not for people living there or work areas, then they were storing something...water, foodstuffs, or now the drugs that had been brought to them to use. As they went to the next level, then the next, Jamey started to see things that she'd not noticed on the lower levels.

"It's words. Like...I don't know. In a language that I know but don't know why." Jamey went to the wall and put her hands over the meticulously drawn pictures. "And I'm not sure, but I think this is written in blood. Dragon's blood."

"I agree." Leo moved back as far as he could, then smiled at her. "It's a message from Bob. He must have put out some kind of beacon for us to come here and see this. Let me see. It says, 'My lady and lord. Good day to you. I have left this for you. To help you to understand that the magic that you hold will now be used for things that even I do not fully understand.'"

"Well that's certainly going to be helpful." Jamey felt her heart ache for the dragon who had written this for them. Asking Leo to continue, she went to the window at the end of the hall and looked out over the large area behind the building.

"'As you have surmised, you can fly. I do not believe that will be as helpful to you as some of the things that I have given you, but it might serve you well. I must confess that there is no way for me to know how much magic you shall get from me, but it will be a great deal.'" Leo leaned back against the wall and looked toward her as he spoke. "This isn't what I had in mind when I told you I wanted you."

"And what did you have in mind, Leo? Sex again?" He nodded and grinned at her. "Is that all men think about? How to have sex? Where to have it, and let's not forget the different ways there are to have it?"

"If you come here I'll show you just what kind of things I think about when it comes to sex and you." Jamey felt her body warm up and her nipples tighten in her bra. "I can smell you from here. Take off your clothing and come here. I believe you said something about sucking my cock."

Jamey moved toward him, thinking about his body and how much she wanted it. Her clothing seemed to disappear and had she not been so needy, it might have freaked her out a bit. But Leo's disappeared as well and his cock seemed to be calling to her. And she was not one to turn down a call from her mate.

Chapter 13

Master roared out his frustrations. Rocks tumbled around him as the mountain shook. He had failed. Not only had his greatest plan ever had failed him, but they had fucking hurt him again. And this time he was pretty sure that he might not recover from it. Looking down at the wound in his leg, he could see bone and muscle.

"They will pay." He roared again, though softer. Master didn't want the entire mountain to come down on his head. "Though right now it would not surprise me should it do that. I cannot win with these people. Why not?"

Randall was dead. Master wasn't sure how he felt about that. He didn't care for the man, not in the slightest, but he'd been someone to talk to. Closing his eyes, he made his way to the other realm and to the lab where Dolin was working…whining mostly, but he was supposed to be working as well.

He was a mess as well. His legs been…well, chewed to nothingness. He had a stump on his right leg, but he whined so much about the pain in it that Master wanted to take his head off as well. As soon as he realized that he was there, Dolin cringed from him.

"Fix my leg." Dolin nodded, and using a wheelchair that he'd procured from the other realm, he rolled to the large first aid kit that lay on the lab table. "Randall is dead."

Dolin dropped the roll of gauze in his hand and turned to him. There was disbelief there as well as joy. Master sat on one of the tables to have him look at and repair his leg.

"What killed him? I have heard that they have bombs there. Large ones that can take out entire worlds. And they have them just sitting around in things called silos. Why they would mix a bomb with their grain is beyond me, but they are only humans and far less smart than we." Master cared nothing for things that did not benefit him and didn't answer Dolin. He had no idea what they had. "I must say that I had hoped that this would happen, but I would have enjoyed being there to watch it."

His hand went out and hit Dolin before he could think to check his strength. Christ, the man was the most annoying thing he'd ever encountered. And as old as he was, Master had come across a few more than most. But when Dolin landed, he knew his mistake immediately.

Things had been broken for a while now. Thanks to the temper that Randall had on a daily basis, things were not up to the usual standards in the lab. Broken furniture accounted for most of the debris, but glass doors had also been shattered, as well as glass front cabinets. This is what Dolin had hit when Master struck him.

His head was lying precisely between what was left of his thighs. His body hung mostly out of the cabinet, but his arm dangled slightly and it looked like he was waving at him. The look on his face made Master laugh.

Dolin looked relieved. And while that was bad enough, the fact that he'd been holding onto the bandage that would help cover Master's wound made Master start to giggle. Then his laughter got the better of him until he was lying down on the table holding his belly.

None of this was funny. Not only was it not funny, but it was likely going to delay things for him in a way that would make it so that Master was going to lose all the momentum that he'd gained with Randall. He stood up and went to the dead man.

"You've really messed things up for me." He pulled out his dick, a useless thing for the most part, and pissed on the man. "I told you I'd do this. Warned you that someday that I would piss on your dead body. And here it is."

Master went back to the table after he'd emptied himself. He had no idea how to use the things in the box, so he started putting things on his leg that he thought might work. Master squirted the first tube that he picked up all over the open wound, and started screaming at the pain immediately.

He couldn't get it off him quickly enough. The burning, the pain of it, nearly made him grab a knife and cut his leg open more to get rid of the foul smelling ointment. The fact that it smelled of camphor should have warned him, but he'd been pissed and had hurried through it.

"Christ, will nothing ever turn out right for me?" He didn't think so, and his question to Dolin, of course, had gone unanswered. Master limped over to the head and picked it up by the hair. "You have done me wrong, Dolin. You and Ward have gotten off much too easily for you to be dead and me suffering. I want my revenge on Rembrandt. I need it."

After he'd gotten his leg to stop throbbing, he sat down and decided his best course of action was to seal the wound up. He took water bottles that seemed to be in abundance in the place and poured it over his sore leg until he couldn't stand the pain any longer. Not touching the small vials of drugs nor the tubes of flaming pain, he pulled out a small package of thread and a needle.

It took him nearly five hours to get his leg sewn up. It might have taken him less time had he had any idea what he was about, but as it was, he was quite pleased with the results. It was sloppy and the stitches puckered up, but he was no longer looking at a gaping hole, and that satisfied him greatly.

Picking up the head, he walked around the little town. There wasn't a soul around. And not only that, but the place looked as if someone had been tearing things up just for spite. He looked into the lifeless eyes of Dolin.

"That would be Randall. He never was a good person. I would imagine that he wasn't a good child either. I wasn't." Master looked around the street that he knew Ward had lived on. "Such destruction. You should see what he did to your home. Much more than I did, let me tell you. Should you like to see it?"

Turning at the next street, he found several houses that were in good shape and moved through them, picking up things that he liked, breaking things that seemed to be useless. When he found a picture of a family, something in his mind made him study the picture hard, and that was when he turned to Dolin again. Showing him the picture, he nodded to it and then looked at Dolin.

"Do you know this man? I think I do but I can't think right now." Master smashed the picture and then took out the photo and put it in the bag he'd found earlier. "I'm pretty sure that I should know him, but I can't place him right now."

As he moved through the houses, he continued to talk to Dolin. It occurred to him that someone might think him insane, but he knew better. It was just a way to bide his time, and to not be so lonely.

"Who would have thought that I'd be lonely? I spent most of my time as a human alone. Not that people wouldn't have anything to do with me, but just because I liked my own company. Remy was forever around people. I thought them to suck him dry, but he didn't mind."

Remy was a good man according to everyone back then. He'd been a sap so far as Master knew. "He would just lend you money if he had it. Some said he'd have given the shirt off his back, should he have one on. Most of the time he would work without one. Bronzed God is what some of the people called him. Pfft. He was a sap."

As he wandered over to the next street, picking up items as he went, Master thought of the day that he'd had Remy's family killed. Remy had been right about his involvement in it. He'd only watched from a distance, not even close enough to hear the screams. But he'd gone there later, after the house was burned down.

"She lay there, her clothing all gone and her skin as raw as my own wound. There were no children about that I could see. She'd done something with them, though at the time, I had no clue about the shelter under her." Master had even gone to the barn after the fire there was burned out as well. "His horses, all of them prized, had died. Some, two that I know of, were not even his. He'd been caring for them. But did the people get upset? Nay, they did not. They only mourned his losses.

"To think…well, I know that you are unable to do that now, but I did think about how they would have strung me up should they have known my part in the ordeal." He could have stopped the men who had gone to Remy's house. Or at least have gotten some of the town's people together and made a production about finding the men who had done this. "But why should I have cared a fig for his family? He was not a man that I liked even then. Remy was a man that expected things from you."

All he'd wanted from him was for Master to help out around Remy's farm to repay the money he'd loaned him. Master had never been in a position to pay him back, not that he would have. But Remy wanted him to come by his home and help with the hogs, or the horses. Master had been too busy for such things.

"I had my own way of living. I still do, as a matter of fact. It didn't involve me going around slopping hogs or taking hay to horses. Then or now." He'd never understood the reason for giving hay to horses. Just put them in a field and let them go. That should have been more than enough. "And that wife of his. She had offered to show me my letters and numbers. Why would a man like me need to know his letters?"

It might have come in handy a few times, Master thought. And then today with the kit. He might have been able to see what he was putting on his skin rather than burning his leg nearly off. It hadn't been that bad, but it had hurt. But learning was something else that he'd never had a desire for.

He showed Dolin his house and then made his way over to Ward's. They'd had really pretty homes, he supposed, but right now they looked like messes. Someone—he figured it had been Randall—had destroyed them beyond what Master had done to them. As he made his way back to the lab he thought of all the things that had come to him. Not a lot of it had turned out the way he'd wanted, but some had. He looked at the bag that he'd carried around and all the jewels that he'd collected. He knew, just from experience, that they'd be worth more in the other realm than they had been here. He looked at Dolin again.

"Do you go or stay?" No answer. Of course he was going to go. Just to keep him company, Master thought. "I'm not crazy. I know that you're dead and that you're not really anyone I'm talking to, but you're going to go with me. There is nothing left here that I need return for."

So willing himself back to the cave, Master thought about how he was going to get some money. He knew that was going to be the factor in making sure that Remy and his band of blood brothers were ended.

~~~

Leo was not paying attention. He knew that he should have been, but all he could think about was Jamey and the things that she'd done to him and he'd done to her earlier today. Christ, it was like they were sexual deviants or something. And now he had to sit here and try to listen to what was going on, but his mind drifted again to her.

As soon as she'd dropped to her knees in front of him, he should have known that it wouldn't be a simple blow job with her. She'd taken him into her mouth and had done things with her tongue that had made him hang onto the wall or fall over from the sheer pleasure of it. Her hot, wet mouth had been a haven, one that he'd never thought to leave until she sucked him down past the tight muscles of her throat and begged him to fuck her this way.

Leo moved in and out of her mouth slowly at first, wanting to enjoy her for as long as he could. He did know that since he'd been changed, his stamina was a great deal more than it had been. But with her, it had been never-ending. Not even when he came down her throat had he had enough, but when she stood up, Leo knew a new kind of pleasure.

Her fingers seemed to be everywhere on his body. His back, his ass, even his toes were touched by her. He had been told to not touch her, to let her explore, and Leo had thought it would be easy. Never had he thought that she'd take him to places that he'd never return from.

"Let me suck your breast." Her head said no but he could see the desire in her face. "Please? I need to taste that sweet hard nubbin."

"No. Not yet. I want you so desperate for me that you take me hard. I want to feel you fucking me at the back of my throat again, but with your cock in my pussy." He told her he was nearly there now. "No, you're not. Not even close."

Spreading out his arms and hands, his wings seemed to quiver too. When she told him to close his eyes, he felt a puff of air and looked up. Somehow they were in their bedroom. Leo asked her how she'd done that.

"I just thought of us there. And you tied to the bed." Lifting his arms up, he realized that not only was he tied to the bed by his arms but his ankles as well. "See how hard you are? I'm going to have so much fun with you before I let you go."

"Do I get to return the favor sometime?" She'd told him she was counting on it. "Good, because for as long as you make me wait to fuck you, I'm going to do it twice as long to you."

Leo watched her as she touched him more, her hands and mouth doing things to him that had him begging for her to let him go. His cock was so hard it ached. His cream was dripping down to his groin in great streams of hot cum.

"Suck me, Jamey. Give me some relief." She not only didn't touch him but ignored his cock for his belly. Her long hair curled around him, making him beg her again and again for a climax. When she sat over him, her pussy inches from his cock, he looked up at her. "Take me. And let me hold you."

"I want to ride you." Her body lowered over his. His cock wasn't just swallowed up by her heat but seemed to become a part of her. Leo pulled at the ropes, felt them dig into his flesh as she rode him slowly. "You're so thick right now. It's like I have two dicks in my pussy, you have me so stretched out."

"Jamey, please baby." Leo rocked his hips up, trying his best to get her to come so he could. He knew that when she tightened around him, he was going to come hard enough to see stars if he survived this at all. "Let me come, baby. I hurt to fill you."

Her ride seemed to take on a new level of torture. Her hands on his chest now, she played with his nipples, tugging at them hard enough that he cried out with it. It didn't hurt, not at all, but the pleasure of it was nearly too much. When her mouth joined her hands, he did cry out and told her he was going to come if she bit him again.

"Leo?" Leo looked at the person in front of him. His mind had been lost in a haze of sexual fun and he couldn't have said who the person was if his life depended on it. But his laughter got him. Davis. Davis had brought him from his memories of he and Jamey before he'd come here today.

"I was thinking and got caught up in it. Sorry." Davis laughed harder. "Christ, she's going to kill me. I've never had a woman who could...is Vicki like this succubus? I mean, seriously sexy and a killer in bed?"

"Not just in bed, but anywhere she can find me alone." Leo nodded. Looking around the room, he realized that they were alone. "I needed to talk to you. Remy was called away on business. I think that he saw the sappy look on your face and decided that it was a lost cause and went to find Skylar."

Leo flushed but told him he'd help any way he could. "Oh, did you hear that the last guy showed up last night? I've not met him, have you?"

"Yes. That's what I wanted to talk to you about. His name is Nathaniel. He goes by Nate. He's a bitter bastard. I'm not sure what his story is, and Hector isn't saying, but Remy and he got into a fight last night almost as soon as he walked in the door." He asked him about what. "Something about him not wanting to be here. That he had more important things to do than to kill malefactors. I don't think that was what he was really pissy about, but something else. As soon as he saw Hector, he punched him in the face, and had Vicki and Skylar not been there, I think he might have tried to kill him. He refuses to come out of his room for any reason. And Chris said that he's a shifter, but is not sure what kind."

Leo wondered what the guy's story was. He'd not wanted to be here either, but this guy was violent about it. That just didn't make him want to get to know the guy at all. Not that it sounded like he was going to get the chance anyway. But he thought he'd like to go and talk to the man sooner rather than later.

The decision was taken out of his hands when the man walked into the room with him a few minutes after Davis had left him. He just stared at him for several seconds before he sat down at the computer and started playing around with it. Leo decided that he'd treat him like he would one of his students, ignore him until he spoke first.

"This place...what can you tell me about it?" Leo didn't move when asked, figuring that he'd play the man too. "I'm not really thrilled about being here, but it was come here or the nightmares wouldn't stop."

"What sort of nightmares?" Nate shrugged but did look at him. "Do you expect me to answer you and you not me? It doesn't work that way around here. What sort of nightmares?"

He didn't think he was going to answer him. Nate had a look on his face that Leo thought looked resigned. But Leo could see the fear there too...underlying sure, but it was there. When he looked away, Leo knew this was hard on him.

"There's a woman. I don't know her, and even if I do in the dream, I honestly don't know who she is or what she is to me. Then there's this creature. He takes her from me. Again, I'm not sure if she actually means anything to me or not, but it's there, this deep in the gut feeling that she's more than just a passing fuck buddy." Leo asked him if it was his mate. When he looked at him, Leo could see that he thought perhaps she was. "He takes her, this creature. And when he does, she's...he eats her. Rips her in half with these teeth that are long and sharp like a dragon's, but he's not one. I try to save her, but there just isn't any way for me to get to her."

"Who else is there? Can you see any of them?" Nate nodded but said nothing. "Us. All of us are there. But what is happening that we can't help you?"

"You're all dead."

Leo wasn't sure what to say to him. Or even if he knew what to say to him. Nate started working on the computer as they both sat there and Leo just let his mind work around what he'd said. Then something occurred to him.

"You said that we're all dead. Are we headless?" Nate looked at him oddly. "It's the only way to kill us. I mean most of us. You? I have no clue, but the rest of us…. Did you get anything from Hector? A mark or sigil that you didn't have before?"

When Nate sat there for several seconds, Leo wasn't sure that he'd understood what he was saying. But when he stood up and pulled his shirt off and turned, he could see that he'd been branded as well. But his tat was different in several ways.

His back was seriously marked. It looked more like an entire scene rather than just a single animal like his was. Getting up, he went to have a closer look and fell back against the nearby table.

"It's us." Nate told him that it changed all the time. "What do you mean it changes all the time? It moves?"

"Pretty much. And the people change. When I first noticed this thing, and only because my back was itching like a son of a bitch, the others weren't there. Rick and Chris. And yeah, I knew their names as soon as they showed up. The women, just Vicki and Skylar until about a week ago. Then I knew Jamey's name. I think it's a fucking mess that I have this shit."

"Do you know what it means?" He didn't expect him to know. It was the thing around here. Mostly learning by their mistakes. And the things they could do as well. So when he had no idea, Leo just nodded. "Is there any kind of shit you can do? Like, I don't know, do you have wings?"

"No. Should I?" Leo brought his out and smiled when Nate backed away. "Fuck, that is really messed up. Can you actually fly with them?"

"Yeah. And we've reasoned out that as soon as we get our mates that they come to us. At least that's the theory. We're sort of figuring this out as we go too."

"In answer to your earlier question, I've been thinking about it and I don't know if you're beheaded or not. When I wake up, I just know that you're all dead and I'm in shit up to my ears. This woman is dead because of something that I did or didn't do, and it's all going to go to hell in a hand basket and it's all my fault."

"I doubt it's all your fault. We've been fucking up royally as we go along, like I said. Two weeks ago we tried to take out a system that we were sure was supplying energy to the malefactors, and it turned out to be an electrical panel. Damned near took out the entire neighborhood." There were other things too, like the warehouse. They needed to figure out how to bring in more supplies or figure out a way to grow more. They had more people there than they could feed. "We need help. Not just from you but from everyone. Remy is doing the best he can, but the man can only do so much."

"I'm not going to join this merry group of men." Leo just nodded and started to turn back to his chair. Nate spoke again. "I'm not. I have to get my own shit together, and this place is not what I had in mind."

"You think any of us had this in mind? Do you think that perhaps we all banded together and thought, hey, let's get aliens from another planet to come here, kill most of the people we know, and then see what sort of fucked-up shit we can have done to ourselves? Christ, man, get your fucking head out of your ass and be realistic. If you don't want to help, then I would suggest that you pack your shit and move on. Or, like Hector said you might do, kill yourself. We've no time nor the energy to baby a whiney-assed, fucking selfish bastard like that."

Nate stood up, and Leo let a little of himself go. The dragon that had been there before but had been absent until right this second appeared again. He could feel him run along his body like he was a part of him. And Leo wasn't surprised when he felt Jamey come up behind him.

"There a problem here?" Remy stood just in the doorway behind Nate. No one moved and Remy stayed where he was. "I can feel the shift in power around you. The dragon?"

"I think he's here. With us." Jamey nodded. "We're him now. And this guy is just leaving. I'll help him."

Nate simply left them. He didn't speak to anyone and didn't answer Remy when he asked him if he needed help packing. When he left, Leo pulled Jamey into his arms and held her. The dragon calmed a little.

"You're a dragon now, the two of you are." Leo nodded, and Remy just stared at him before turning as he continued. "Write it on the board with the other shit." Leo and Jamey just laughed. They were going to need a bigger board before long.

Chapter 14

"He's not leaving." Jamey looked at Leo when he spoke. They'd been in the living room for about twenty minutes just sitting on the couch, not speaking. "I talked to him a bit ago again, and he said that he can't leave. The pain in his head gets bad when he gets near the line with the intentions of parting from us."

"I don't think I'm going to trust him to hold up my back." Leo just shrugged. "What is it about him that makes you trust him? You do too, don't you?"

"He reminds me of me when I first got here. I wasn't nearly as bad, but almost. But he has this added burden of knowing that…well, thinking that we're all going to die. I asked him to pay more attention to the stuff going on around him when he dreams again." Jamey wondered how that was going to work out when Leo spoke again. "He knows the story like he's reading it from a book. The outcome and the people are always the same, except that you came into the story a few weeks ago. The details to him are the same, but he needs to look at the picture."

"Makes sense I guess." She looked down at where their bodies were touching and thought that they should talk about the dragon. He had disappeared, Remy had said. As soon as he was dead, he was just gone. She wondered where he'd gone and had a feeling he had come to the two of them. But it didn't seem that either of them were ready for that when Leo spoke again.

"Do you suppose that his tat on his back is like a movie when things are going on? I mean, we could watch it as it happened?" That was just too fucked up to think about. "I mean, it's worth a try, right?"

"No. I'm not going to be in this guy's bedroom in the hopes that his back suddenly turns into this IMAX kind of movie for me to see how we all are supposed to die. Thanks, but no thanks." Leo laughed at her, and she stood up. "I have to go and find Vicki. She and I are going to work on some things for the school. I would ask you to help, but you have a hard-on right now that makes me crazy, and I don't have time for that."

"Sure you do." Leo stretched out on the couch and she moaned. "Come here. I love it when you ride me. The last time you made me suffer so much that I don't think I could see well for hours."

"You make me crazy." Leo nodded, and she moved toward him. "Okay, but nothing but sex. I'm serious about this school thing."

"Let me school you on some things." When he pulled her atop him, she let him. Her body was on fire for his as well. "I want you all the time, Jamey. Not just for sex, though that is fantastic, but for everything. I don't think I can breathe without your scent in my nose. My heart doesn't beat as well without you in it. I love you."

Jamey looked at him. He'd said that to her before, but there was no way that he loved her. He was just saying it because.... "Why? Why now after all this time are you suddenly falling in love with me?"

"I didn't." Jamey started to pull away from him, but he held her tight. "What I mean is, I didn't just fall in love with you. I would like to say that I was brooding it over, but to be honest with you, I think I was just fucking stupid. I have loved you since the first time I saw you. You're brave, smart, and beautiful, but I was too blind in my...I guess misery to see anything beyond the pain I was in. I'm sorry for that. Profoundly so."

"You hurt me." He nodded as if he knew and kissed her gently on the mouth. "That does not make up for the fact that you shoved me away when we could have been having glorious sex all this time instead of you having your head up your ass."

"We have the rest of our lives to have sex, but to be honest with you, I'd rather make love to you. All the time. Every day for the rest of our lives. And according to Hector, that's a very long time." Jamey let him kiss her again before she lifted her head and looked at him. "Will you marry me?"

She smiled at him before answering. "Will there be a ring? A big fat diamond that I can show off to...? Wait, we have no friends other than the people here. So...yeah, I guess I'll marry you. But I want to have a ring. A pretty one."

Leo reached for the newspaper that he'd had when she came in. She knew that there wasn't anyone printing new ones, so the one he had would have been months old. But he'd been reading it like he was catching up. When he took her hand into his, she sat up when he told her to.

"I was amazed that we're still getting paid. So I went to Hector to see what was going on with that. I was told by one of the people from his realm that there was no one left save a few people hiding in the mountains there. Anyway, he told me that there is a program that pays us. It manufactures what we need in the form of money and then sends it here. I think there was some mention of magic, but I was set on asking him something about that and missed something." He kissed her fingers and then opened her palm. "We worked with something in the office and he had them make me something that I requested. The rest of the money, mostly in diamonds I might add, is stashed with the rest of the stuff I got in a huge case in our room. But this came with it."

Leo dropped the ring into her palm. Jamey was speechless. It was by far the most beautiful ring she'd ever seen. Picking it up with just her little finger, she stared at it.

The entire band was about half an inch wide. The silver of it made her think that was what it was made of, but he told her it was platinum. The jewels that surrounded it, all cut deeply within the surface, were small but formed the most beautiful design that she'd ever seen. It was her dragon.

"I had it made before he...before he came to us after he died. I thought since he brought us together, that it was only fitting that he be a part of our lives for the rest of it. The magic that made this got his image from my mind. I think it's good of him." Jamey nodded, still staring at it. "You have to answer me, Jamey. Or is it that you don't like it? I'm sure that we can—"

Jamey cut him off by kissing him. When she lifted her head, the tears in her eyes blurred her vison of him, but he wiped them away with his thumb. He begged her not to cry.

"I love you too." This time he smiled at her and it seemed to light up his entire face. "And this ring is perfect. I love it so much. We won't be changing a thing about it."

"I'm glad to hear you say that. Because I have one that matches it." He pulled the matching ring out to lie in her palm. Her small ring fit inside of his larger one like her heart did to his. He grinned at her when she told him that. "I was really worried about whether or not it would hurt us should we shift, and so I tried mine on. It seems that like our clothing, it absorbs into our bodies. But Remy said that there was a shine there on my hand that wasn't there before."

He kissed her until she was so hot that he helped her pull her shirt off. They had discovered before that they could easily make their clothing disappear, but there was something so romantic about him stripping her down. As he pulled her bra off, unclasping the hook in the front, she curled her fingers into his hair and willed them to their room. He grinned at her when he lifted his head.

"I take it the talk about schools is off for the time being." She told him it was and it was all his fault. "I will gladly take the fall for you not being there. But right now, I'd very much like to lay you out and taste you."

Lying in the center of the bed, she noticed two things almost immediately. The room was larger by a great deal, and there were windows where there shouldn't have been. But just before she asked him about it, he pulled her pussy to his mouth and bit down on her clit.

~~~

Leo loved it when she came in his mouth. She filled him with so much of her juices that he had to swallow quickly or miss a great deal of it. And the way her hips rode his mouth made his cock hard with need, and he reached down now to free himself. Jamey cried out her second climax just as his cock filled his hand.

He devoured her for as long as she'd let him, which wasn't nearly long enough. But when she begged him to fuck her, he wasn't a man to turn her down. As he made his way up her body, Leo bit her and then licked the tiny wounds closed with his tongue. Christ, she tasted like the best kind of chocolate and the finest wine he'd ever had. When he was near her breast, instead of taking the entire orb into his mouth as he wanted, he pulled just the hard tip into his mouth and chewed on it. Her reaction was more than he could have hoped for.

Her body bowed up off the bed as she wrapped her fingers around him. His cock, already sensitive and full, seemed to know that what he had wrapped around him was enough for now, and emptied onto her body as she came, screaming out his name. Leo wrapped his hand around his cock with her hand and fisted himself until he was hard again. It didn't take as long as he'd thought.

"Take me." He moved his crown over her entrance and was soaked for his efforts. "Take me, Leo, please? I need you inside of me."

Slamming forward, he buried himself to his groin and then stilled. She rode him hard, her body meeting his over and over until he finally couldn't wait any longer. Leo started to pound her hard even as she wrapped her legs over his and met him stroke for stroke. When he came this time, Leo nuzzled her neck and then bit down on her pounding pulse as she screamed her release again and again. Leo emptied into her once again just before dropping over her in exhaustion.

"We sure know how to mess up a bed." Leo rolled to his back and pulled her over him. He laughed when she moaned and continued talking to her gently as she lay there. "I love you so much. I want to spend the rest of my life right here in this bed with you."

The alarm going off had them both jumping up from the bed. He was dressed before her and pulling on his shoes when she paused. Leo stood up, one shoe in his hand, the other on his foot, and looked around the room as she was.

"There is someone...I can't see who it is clearly, but there is someone out there. They're not...I don't know what they are, but they want to come here, but don't trust us. She's reaching out to anyone to see if we can hear her."

"Who?" When she didn't answer him, he reached out and put his hand over hers. He could feel her too. The woman should have been able to cross the line, but for some reason was waiting. "Can you talk to her?"

"Yes. She isn't coming yet. She...she said that there are others, a few like her that need to trust more than just her word before they come beyond the boundaries. I've asked her what we can do to win her trust and she laughed at me." Leo could feel Jamey's frustrations but waited for her to continue. "She's not human. I don't know what she is, but not human at all."

"Vampire." Leo had no idea why he knew that, but it seemed right. "Tell her that one of her kind is here now. Don't tell her his name."

"She knows him. Or of him. There are others that she's sending us. Cats and wolves. She said that they can help us with the power issues and the phones." When Jamey opened her eyes and looked at him, Leo could see the fear there. "She's had dealings with Hector too."

"She's one of us then?" Jamey told him she had no idea. "Do you know what she looks like? Perhaps we can go out and find her, talk her into coming to us or something."

"She's gone. Or at least gone from me being able to talk to her." As she pulled on her shirt and Leo finished pulling on his boots, Jamey told him the rest. "She's old. Not like Remy old, but close. And she said that Rick is as well. That with his age, he has a great deal of powers that they need to heal. What do we do now?"

"Tell Remy and the others." Jamey nodded but didn't look convinced. "If she comes here, someone is going to have to be here. Did she tell you her name? Anything about her?"

"All she said was to be looking for the cats and wolves on the morrow. She said it like that too, on the morrow. And that some of them were sick, but not with anything that would harm us. I didn't think that shifters could get sick."

"Neither did I." They made their way to the command center and were the last to arrive. Remy was telling them that they'd found another one of the sub-machines a town over and that there were a lot of malefactors there.

"Also, Jake thinks that their number is no longer increasing. He's not saying that we're out of the woods just yet, but it doesn't seem to him that any more of the creatures are being made. That is the best news I've had all year." Remy looked around after asking if anyone had anything to add before they headed out, and Jamey raised her hand. After telling them all she knew, Remy nodded. He looked so tired that Leo was beginning to worry about him.

"We'll keep an eye out like she said, but without her coming in here, there's not much we can do." Remy and the others headed out when Vicki stopped them.

"I felt her too. And you're right about her being a vamp. But I asked Rick about it, and he said that the only vampires that he knew that was as old as him were dead or buried until this was over." Leo nodded and asked if she had felt her, or did she speak to her first? "I heard from her. She said that she was...she told me that she won't come here for fear of being trapped. Being a vamp, I'm sure that's a fear for them all."

As they left the compound via the skies, Leo had a moment of wonder to think she was maybe a mate to one of the men that were there now. It would make sense that she was Rick's mate, her being a vampire too, but he'd bet anything that it mattered little what you were when it came to being in love. As he passed over the crowds of malefactors, he looked for someone out of place and didn't see anyone. Leo made his way to the other town just as the rest of them were sitting down on the ground there.

He was stunned by the amount of malefactors. And their colors. There were some faded ones, a few of the blue ones, but a great many of them were in full color and in their own clothing. Then it occurred to him. Newborns. All of these guys were newborns.

"Hector needs to be here. He thinks he might have something that will change them back. Skylar has gone to get him." Leo nodded at Remy. "We're to wait. I don't care for waiting. Waiting can get you killed."

He was right, it could. But they did as they were asked to do while the malefactor's newbies started to pop into their uniforms. It was a frightening thing to see, and he nearly missed what Jamey said to him as he watched as one at a time they moved from brightly colored tee-shirts to drab gray. Leo asked her to repeat it.

"I said, they're bringing them to here to change. I wonder what draws perfectly…well, not really sane humans, but people here to be slaughtered like cattle." Leo started to tell her he had no idea, but then he saw them.

"Look there. At the beginning of the first line. They're getting food. They're promising them food." As he watched, a bag of what appeared to be milk, flour, and other essentials were being handed to each person. "I wonder if they realize that they have no use for it after they're changed."

"Doubtful. But I don't think that's the point. I think that one person from a family is getting the food, handing it off to a family member, then taking the change willingly." As Leo watched, a boy of about ten took the bag from an older man and woman and ran off. "Do you think that they're doing this like this so that they can go back later and get the rest of the family? Surely they know where they lived."

It was like they were lining them all up for the slaughter. The boy stopped just beyond the line of people and watched. He had to know what was going on. Living around here would make it next to impossible not to know. But when his family walked into the building, he turned and ran away. Leo could see the tears in his eyes. Leo decided that when Hector got there, he was going to have him try the serum on those people first. If he could keep track of them afterwards.

Hector arrived a few minutes later. Leo had kept track of the people as best he could, but he'd lost them twice in the shuffle. When he tried to get them to come with him, it was all he could do without harming them to get them to stand still. Christ, he hoped this worked.

"We might have to do this several times over the next few weeks. Just to see if we can get it to work or not." Leo nodded and realized that Hector was afraid. "I mean, one dose might not do a thing to them, and they might still be a killing thing."

"I trust you, Hector." He did too. Leo trusted all of them more than he thought possible. "Just give it to her and let's see what happens. They're changing them faster than we can get them away."

Remy had suggested that they herd the people away, those not yet changed anyway. He'd had a thought to offer them food, but Vicki pointed out that they had the food there while their promises meant nothing. It was hard enough saving who they could without them thinking they were just as bad with their empty promises too.

Hector administered the shot to the woman. His hands had been shaking so hard that Leo was afraid that he'd hit him with the needle rather than the woman. But when she got it, she just stared at them like malefactors normally did. Dead eyes and blank looks.

When her body began to shake, Hector stepped back. He didn't need to get himself hurt, and the woman was shaking hard enough now that Leo wasn't surprised that her bones, her arm, and ankle broke. It was a sight that was sickening as well as fucking scary. When she bowed up, her body nearly in half on the ground where Leo had lain her, he knew that she'd broken her back as well as a few ribs. The sound of it had Hector turning away and moving back as far as he could.

It didn't work. Hector was so disappointed that it was palpable. When Jamey went to him, putting her arm around him, Leo picked up the dead woman and put her with the rest of the bodies that had not gone through the change well. Leo stood over them, looking at the long line of them.

He knew that he should have been helping Remy and the others. But he felt broken too. So much death and for no reason other than money. When he felt someone come to stand beside him, he didn't even look at the person as he began to speak.

"Those children—because I have no doubt that they're all children that are taking this food—will not have anyone to protect them from the people who are supposed to be there to protect them. Not that they don't think this is a way to go, but it's going to not end the way they want." He glanced over to see Rick standing beside him. "I guess you've seen a great deal of shit like this in your life."

"I have. None as cruel as this, but yes. Men and women would give their lives for their children. Some would go to prison for a loaf of bread. Others would starve themselves just to give their own a meal, meager as it might be. But there are those, too, that would steal from their child to satisfy themselves first and foremost. Fathers would beat them when they were simply too young or too sick to work, while the father did not. But this, Leo, this is beyond that and more." They stood there for several minutes before Rick spoke again. "You will live many lifetimes from now on. I will as well, and we will see changes that will not just make our hearts hurt with the pain of it, but we will become jaded in our feelings. I have done so myself."

"I don't want to not feel for anyone." Rick nodded. "You need to find your mate, Rick. She'll make things come into focus for you. Jamey did me."

"I have had a mate, young Leo. She was the light of my life. The woman dreams are made from. But, alas, she has gone on without me. A human, a man, killed her one night to bring me to my knees." Leo started to ask him what happened to her when Rick continued. "There will not be another like her. I am...I am set in my ways and no woman will want to take me on. With no part of my heart to give another, I will live my life alone until I am able to meet the sun again."

"That's how Hector found you. You were trying to meet the sun." Rick said nothing and Leo nodded. "I think if something happened to Jamey, I'd want to die as well."

"You will wish it. There is no greater pain than to lose the one that has your heart in her hands." Rick put his hand on his shoulder as he continued. "We must go. The others are awaiting us. And young Jamey is going to burn the dead here so that no one will come across this massacre."

Leo helped her. The dragon in him came easily, and the two of them rode the winds while taking care of the scene below them. In minutes, there were no traces of the dead, and nothing left of the malefactors that had killed them. Leo headed home with his mate and decided that he was going to work with the children in the new school, if for no other reason than they were life when he was near so much death any other time.

Before You Go...

Share your voice and help guide other readers to these wonderful books. Even if it's only a line or two your reviews help readers discover the author's books so they can continue creating stories that you'll love. Login to your favorite retailer and leave a review. Thank you.

AWARD WINNING, BESTSELLING AUTHOR

Kathi Barton, author of the bestselling series Force of Nature, lives in Nashport, Ohio with her husband Paul. In addition to writing full time Kathi likes to spend time with her eight grandkids, three children and three children-in-laws. She writes to relax and have fun.

Her muse, a cross between Jimmy Stewart and Hugh Jackman brings them to life for her readers in a way that has them coming back time and again for more. Her favorite genre is paranormal romance with a great deal of spice. You can visit Kathi on line and drop her an email if you'd like. She loves hearing from her fans. aaronskiss@gmail.com.

Follow Kathi on her blog: http://kathisbartonauthor.blogspot.com/

www.ingramcontent.com/pod-product-compliance
Lightning Source LLC
Chambersburg PA
CBHW032127170626
46808CB00006B/2139